Dedalus Europe
General Editor: Timothy Lane

MY FATHER'S HOUSE

MY
FATHER'S
HOUSE

Karmele Jaio

translated by Margaret Jull Costa
& Sophie Hughes

Dedalus

Support for the translation of this book was provided by Acción Cultural Española, AC/E.

AC/E
Acción Cultural
Española

Published in the UK by Dedalus Limited
24-26, St Judith's Lane, Sawtry, Cambs, PE28 5XE
info@dedalusbooks.com
www.dedalusbooks.com

ISBN printed book 978 1 915568 08 3
ISBN ebook 978 1 915568 09 0

Dedalus is distributed in the USA & Canada by SCB Distributors
15608 South New Century Drive, Gardena, CA 90248
info@scbdistributors.com   www.scbdistributors.com

Dedalus is distributed in Australia by Peribo Pty Ltd
58, Beaumont Road, Mount Kuring-gai, N.S.W. 2080
info@peribo.com.au   www.peribo.com.au

First published in Spain in 2020
First published by Dedalus in 2023

La casa del padre copyright Karmele Jaio 2020
Published by special arrangement with the Ella Sher Literary Agency
Translation copyright © Margaret Jull Costa & Sophie Hughes 2023

The right of Karmele Jaio to be identified as the author and Margaret Jull Costa & Sophie Hughes as the translators of this work has been asserted by them in accordance with the Copyright, Designs and Patents Act, 1988.

Printed and bound in the UK by Clays Elcograf S.p.A.
Typeset by Marie Lane

A C.I.P. listing for this book is available on request.

THE AUTHOR

Karmele Jaio writes in Basque and translates her own novels into Spanish. She has written three books of short stories, one of poetry and three novels. This is the second of her novels to be translated into English. Her first novel *Her Mother's Hands* brought her several prizes and was adapted for the cinema. *My Father's House* was awarded the Premio Euskadi de Literatura and was voted the Best Book written in Basque in 2019. Her work has also appeared in various anthologies, including *Best European Fiction* and *The Penguin Book of Spanish Short Stories*.

THE TRANSLATORS

MARGARET JULL COSTA

Margaret Jull Costa has worked as a translator for over thirty years, translating the works of many Spanish and Portuguese writers, among them novelists: Javier Marías, José Saramago, and Eça de Queiroz, and poets: Fernando Pessoa, Sophia de Mello Breyner Andresen, Mário de Sá-Carneiro, and Ana Luísa Amaral. Her work has brought her many prizes, among them the 2008 Pen Book-of-the Month-Club Translation Prize and the Oxford Weidenfeld Translation Prize for *The Maias* by Eça de Queiroz. In 2014, she was awarded an OBE for services to literature.

SOPHIE HUGHES

Sophie Hughes is the translator of over twenty books from Spanish, by Spanish and Latin American writers including Fernanda Melchor, Alia Trabucco Zerán, José Revueltas, and Enrique Vila-Matas. She has been nominated for the International Booker Prize four times, and in 2021 she was awarded the Queen Sofia Spanish Institute Translation Prize for *Hurricane Season* by Fernanda Melchor.

For Iñigo Muguruza

For all new men

"I can't write without a reader. It's precisely like a kiss — you can't do it alone."
                                                                John Cheever

Thank you for being by my side while I was writing this book.

ISMAEL

1

From up on the top of the hill

Gunshots in the hills. You hear them again from where you are, up high. You know, though, that the shots aren't coming from the surrounding trees, but from inside you. Your body is just another part of the greenery. How many empty cartridges must get lost in the undergrowth, like little hearts that slowly corrode over time and yet beat on, and on, and on...

Gunshots in the hills. You've heard them again, from up high. And you can see the cartridges as clearly as if you were holding them in your hand. Trust cartridges, made in Eibar. Your father's watchful gaze as he checks to see if you've loaded them into the shotgun correctly. Red or green, with a gold base, and packed with pellets. The pellets swiftly expand when they pierce the flesh, like some sort of evil spermatozoa. Those stupid cartridges go flying into the bushes and there's no way to retrieve them. Not that anyone really tries. When all's said and done, they're just empty casings. Nobody thinks about how they continue beating and firing — bang, bang, bang — however rusty, however old.

You've reached the top, panting hard, having raced out of

your study, leaving the computer on, and possibly also the hall light. You left without really knowing where you were going, as urgently as a diver furiously swimming up to the surface for air. Propelled more by angst than by the strong southerly wind. A familiar feeling that came back to you at your computer when you remembered yesterday's nightmarish news about the girl found in the woods.

The news about the girl who was raped and abandoned up in the hills. Some hunters found her, too late. It turned your stomach, you can't get it out of your head, it's like what happened in Pamplona all over again, and you really didn't need that. The last straw. What a hackneyed phrase, another tired cliché. No, seriously, you really can't write any more. Your head is one big mess. One day they'll finally find something there, a malignant tumour that prevents you from thinking. That prevents you from writing.

The news about the girl who was raped and abandoned in the woods. You're not sure if it's affected you more because you fear for your daughters — especially now you know that Eider was in Pamplona the night of the tragedy — or because of where it took place. Out in the wild, in the hills, a landscape that still tears at your skin like brambles, a landscape that has haunted your dreams since you were a boy.

And now here, at the top of Olarizu, a brisk forty-minute walk from your house, you ask yourself why your feet have carried you out into the woods. You wonder why the angst you feel has driven you to this precise spot, to the very epicentre of your fears.

You gaze down at the city from above, your thinning hair fluttering about your forehead. Up here, you've finally been able to take a deep breath and calm down a little. There's always something so calming about being up above it all.

You haven't been here since you were a kid. Your father brought you once or twice, soon after you moved to Vitoria, just as he used to take you to Kalamua or Ixua when you lived in Eibar, only without the shotgun. And yet the setting now fills your head with the sound of gunshots. Bang, bang, bang. Gunshots in the hills. Gunshots and dogs barking. For you, there is no more terrifying combination of sounds.

You look at the city that welcomed you when you were fifteen. A city that has grown with you, that has expanded like an ink blot on a piece of paper, losing intensity as the stain widens and spreads. It took you a moment to pinpoint the roof of your parents' apartment building. The Church of San Pedro helped you to place it. They've been living in that apartment since the move from Eibar. Like their fellow residents, who also came from elsewhere: Zamora, Cáceres... In many cases, those neighbours would spend their summers back in their home towns. You remember months of empty apartments, lowered blinds, deserted stairwells. The coolness of the hallway compared to the desert heat of the street. Cold landings and scorching patios. Those intense August contrasts.

At this hour, your mother will be mopping the kitchen floor, as she has done for the last fifty years, from left to right, right to left, zigzagging back and forth as if trying to remove the evidence of a murder. Your mother, always removing evidence, silencing voices, putting out fires. She'll have left the balcony door open so that the floor dries more quickly and to get rid of the smell of cooking. Fried fillet steak and bleach, that post-lunch blend of smells also travelled with you from Eibar to Vitoria. Homes aren't physical places, they're atmospheres that follow us from one house to the next. Nancy has been helping them out ever since your father started losing his memory, but there's no way your mother would let her mop the floor. Nobody mops like her. Mopping is her domain.

To the right of your parents' home is the bell tower of the Church of San Miguel. You lived near there for years, in the old part of town, with Jasone and the girls. But in among that compact jumble of houses, you haven't been able to pinpoint the one that used to be yours. Just as you can't see your daughters either. They've already left the scene, flown the nest. They no longer need your protection. They move in and out of sight like those flocks of birds you often watch in the afternoon from your study window, making shapes and patterns in the sky only to immediately unmake them again.

Your current house, the one where you and Jasone now live just the two of you, albeit with two spare bedrooms for your daughters' comings and goings, is easy to spot. It's in one of the residential areas in the south of the city, where the buildings are more spread out. You can even see the terrace your study looks out on. The window from which you've observed the world in recent years. On the other side of that window is your computer, your dried-up cup of coffee on the desk, your fears, your post-it notes, your paper clips, your slippers beside the chair, your nightmares, your books, your notepads, your world. There is your novel, the one you've been trying to write for the last two years. There is your secret. A novel that isn't progressing, a creative drought, a classic case of writer's block. Never a truer word spoken. Yet another cliché.

16

Just like every sentence you write. Over the last two years, your words have created nothing but cardboard scenery for a stage set. But how to create a really believable set for a world you've always kept well away from in real life. You've lost count of the number of times you've regretted your decision to try and describe the corrosive political atmosphere of the Basque Country in the 1980s. Putting the political conflict at the centre of your work was a disastrous idea. If it hadn't been for Vidarte's review of your last book, you might never have got yourself into this mess. And if it hadn't been for the offer you received to have your next work published in Spanish translation, you might not have embarked on a history of that time of "*Si vis pacem, para bellum*" — "If you want peace, prepare for war" — which was your sister's mantra. You thought the publisher would like that authentic touch, an insider's view of the Basque conflict, but you've regretted it ever since. Over the last two years, you've questioned every single line you've written; not a word of it rings true, because you didn't live through those years the way your sister did, ending up getting arrested, or like Jauregi or countless others. You always ran away from political commitment, from activism; you ran away from the first sign of pain or risk and kept the conflict at arm's length. So how are you supposed to write about it now, if you can't find even fragments of truth in either your hands or your memory.

You can see your study window and it seems so small... Perhaps that's it. Perhaps that's the reason all your ideas have dried up in recent years. You're looking at reality from too far away. You can't see anything from there, detached from the world. Vidarte was right all along. In his review, he wrote that your characters felt like extra-terrestrial beings, that your novel didn't make a single reference to the world in which they live, to the social or political context... He said you never let your characters out in the street, that you kept them locked indoors, between four walls, debating among themselves. But he also said that you'd failed to do even that properly, because you watched them from afar, as if you were afraid to enter their thoughts, their nightmares. In your novel there was no engagement with either the setting or your characters' inner lives. And without any real engagement with the truth, there can be no art. That's what the critic Vidarte wrote about your last novel, along with a few other equally charming comments. And over these last two years you haven't been able to shake off the image of him hovering over your study day and night, calling you an extra-terrestrial. You're an extra-terrestrial, Alberdi.

Perhaps that's the problem. In this new novel, you've tried to get close to the real world, but it isn't easy; whenever you get too close, you take fright — as you did when you heard about that poor girl — and you scurry back to the refuge of your study. It's not easy engaging fully with what's happening in the world, or with the people in it, if you never leave your study from whose window you see only your own nightmares and the geraniums on the balcony that Jasone has been neglecting lately.

You see drought. You see darkness.

Perhaps it's the darkness that has finally driven you up this hill. Yes here. Perhaps it's the darkness that has finally propelled you into the light.

2

Trapped in another time

You ate your breakfast staring at the filter coffee machine. For years you've eaten breakfast sitting opposite the same bloody thing. Jasone has told you countless times that you need to change it, that it doesn't go with the new kitchen, which, with its minimalist furniture and metallic finishes, looks more like a spaceship than a kitchen. The old coffee maker is out of place. At the very least you should buy yourselves one that uses capsules. But you're adamant that no other machine makes coffee as good as this. Even so, for some reason, ever since you changed house and kitchen, you've found that coffee machine somehow discomfiting, as if it were a reflection of you, as if you, too, were out of place, outmoded, out of keeping.

When Jasone goes off to work at the library and you're left on your own in the house, you feel the machine's presence even more strongly. The slow rhythm of the coffee as it drips into the glass jug couldn't be more different from the speed of the news headlines scrolling across the bottom of the screen of the TV you always have on in the background over breakfast each morning: Donald Trump, Aleppo, Lesbos, the Dow Jones, oceans of plastic… No, those news stories are from another planet. Out there, everything moves very fast. Inside, it's just you and the electric coffee machine, trapped in another time. Drip drip dripping, gradually being drained of substance.

For a long time now you've watched only foreign channels: CNN, CBS… It calms you down. The bombs explode somewhere far away. Almost as far away as the bombs in the story you're failing to write. News of rapes that have taken place locally never seem to filter through to those channels. They're never going to tell you about how, in the early hours of that morning, a girl was raped in the very town where your youngest daughter spent the night. Jasone phoned you the second she heard the news.

'I've been calling her, but there's no answer,' she said in an anguished voice. 'I think she's got her phone switched off.'

You instantly regretted having given Eider permission to go to Pamplona.

'All of my friends are going, Dad.'

You can't think how it even occurred to you to let her go. She's only seventeen.

When, after one very long hour, your daughter finally called her mother — 'What's the big deal, my phone died, chill out'— you felt as if you were deflating, as if all the air you'd been holding in were escaping through your mouth. A very long hour. An hour-long rape. Your daughter's rape. You experienced it as if it had really happened, and since then you've felt as if an alarm were going off inside you, as if the mere mention of a man abusing a woman, raping her, murdering her, inflicted a deep wound on you. Now, as when you first heard the news of that girl who was raped and abandoned in the hills (the way someone might toss away their empty cartridges), you feel afraid, terribly afraid for what could happen to your daughters. But your fear is all mixed up with a feeling of guilt, although you can't quite put your finger on where it's coming from. Or perhaps you can, perhaps all Jasone's remarks since she set up her feminist book club — all her 'this is a war', and 'they're killing us' — have left their mark on you. That way of talking about men as if they were all the same. Ever since that awful morning after the San Fermín festivities, you've been paralysed by this mixture of fear and guilt. You've regressed to being the little boy who used to have nightmares about the woods, about the dogs' barking during the frantic, agonising search for your cousin Aitor. In those dreams, too, the fear was always tinged with guilt.

Your old obsessions and your old paralysis have returned. Something in your head isn't working. Something in there has caused your imagination to stagnate and blocked the flow of ideas as you sit at your computer. And not only there. Last week, you completely blanked at the cash machine, unable to remember your pin. You walked away without withdrawing any money. You picture a small black ball inside your skull, a slowly growing tumour, and you're certain that this is what's clouding your mind and preventing you from writing like you used to, gliding from one paragraph to the next, always sure of where you were going, of where you wanted to go.

That black ball is also the cause of your nightmares and the worry that builds and builds inside until you can't stand it any more and have to leave the house and race up to the nearest hilltop. And the worst part is, the doctors can't find anything wrong. But what would today's doctors know?

They're barely older than your daughters. What would they know about illness, about failing bodies and atrophying minds? You hate them even more than you hate young writers, the stupid wave of promising new writers. The doctors tell you there's nothing to worry about. They'll never admit that they're simply incapable of finding anything. They made you a follow-up appointment in six months. Six months. You could die in that time. In that time the little black marble in your head could grow to the size of a ping-pong ball. Or one of those terrifying rubber bullets used by the police.

You've been afraid of dying ever since you were little. Back when you still lived in Eibar, you would pull the sheets up over your head at night — you still associate fear with the musty smell of the sheets in the house in Eibar — and you'd lie there, perfectly still, sweating, afraid that at any moment Death itself would appear in your bedroom. Those fears and nightmares only intensified after your cousin Aitor went missing up in the hills, and half the town spent two whole days and nights looking for him. You and your father included. Even though, by that point, you were already living in Vitoria, you both returned to Eibar to join in the search.

As a boy, whenever you had nightmares, you would jump out of bed and run along the chilly corridor to your sister's room. Tucked up in Libe's bed, you would calm down — her smell calmed you down. Libe has always been braver than you. The big sister. The one who, once you were both older, wasn't afraid of rubber bullets or being arrested. The one who wasn't afraid of getting into the most dangerous political situations, or, trickier still, getting out of them. And get out she did. She ran off on her own to Berlin, where she still lives. That didn't scare her either. Now she's still saving the world in her own way working for an NGO helping refugees.

You, on the other hand, are a coward. And knowing this weighs on you.

When Jasone leaves for work each morning, when you hear the front door slam, the dreaded silence begins. Lately, your mind only produces words that dissolve into mush like wet cardboard. Page after page of notes, sentences that stare back at you the moment you finish writing them, as if to say: 'Is that it?'

The novel you're working on is really a caricature of life during the conflict, a first draft that was dead before it was even born, a story even you don't believe. One big lie. Even more dated and out of place than the filter coffee machine you stare at as you eat your breakfast each morning.

3

Old nightmares

When Jasone gets in from work each day, when you hear the jangle of her keys, you bolt out of your study towards the front door, like a dog who's spent all day cooped up and waiting for its owner to come home. But it's not only Jasone you want. You also crave the freshness of the street that she carries on her clothes and face. The same crisp, clean air visitors bring with them when you're ill. And those cheeks as cold as keys.

Like the cold your father used to bring home with him after a day's hunting. The cold that would enter the house with your father, making your mother's body and face freeze. That way he had of handing her the shotgun for her to put away and his dirty boots to be cleaned. The cold of the water your mother would use to clean them in the bathroom sink. Your mother's red knuckles under the cold water. Her nails torn from scraping out the tiny pebbles embedded in the grips on the soles.

Today, as usual, on hearing the jangle of keys, you leave your study and follow your wife down the corridor while she takes off her coat, as if you are waiting for her to tell you something, as if she were supposed to report back on the outside world: 'Did you see anyone we know? (Did anyone ask after me?) What have you got there?' Like a child, you rummage through the shopping bags she puts down on the kitchen table, looking for something, quite what even you didn't know. A message in a bottle.

'Has your mother been over again?' she asks on seeing the Tupperware containers in the fridge. Jasone eats lunch with her colleagues from the library every day except Friday, while you eat lunch alone from Monday to Thursday, and so are more than happy to accept the croquettes, the tuna or bean stew that your mother brings.

'I've told her to stop, but, I mean... At least it gives her a reason to leave the house.'

'You shouldn't let her.'

'But she loves doing it.'

'You shouldn't let bringing you food be her sole reason for leaving the house. You should talk to your father.'

'To my father? He's hardly in a state to be lectured to.'

Some part of your father's brain has disconnected, and you've convinced yourself that whatever you have must be hereditary, that some families are weaker, more vulnerable to disease than others. You've convinced yourself that something is about to explode inside you at any moment, probably that black ball.

Jasone sighs as she lights the little incense sticks by the front door on her way to the bedroom. She always does the same when she arrives home from work, before changing out of her clothes. Lighting incense is her way of telling you that the house smells musty. Of old men.

'Do you know when my next appointment is? Guess,' you say, raising your voice so she can hear you in the bedroom, all the while still rifling through the supermarket bags, which are wet from the rain.

'Are you still going on about the neurologist?' she replies, returning from the bedroom, now changed out of her work clothes.

She opens the fridge, takes out a lettuce and a large tomato, and starts preparing a salad for supper. She tells you not to worry, that once you've finished the book, all your ailments will disappear, that you always suffer from aches and pains when you're writing, and that there's nothing wrong with your head. And she slices the tomato in two with such precision that it looks like she's dissecting a brain. You stand there staring at the heart of the tomato, as if looking for a tumour.

Jasone doesn't understand that this time it's different. You haven't told her about what happened at the cashpoint, or about the nightmares that have come back with a vengeance. The same nightmares you had when you were young, only now it's not your cousin Aitor asking for your help among the brambles. The setting hasn't changed — the woods, the rain, the sheer drop. Now it's a woman asking you for help. A man is shaking her and pulling down the straps of her tank top to expose her breasts. You see the terror in the woman's eyes, you see her screaming, but you can't hear her voice. You can only read her lips begging you for help. And you do nothing. You're afraid. The way leading up to the woman is very steep and muddy, you could slip and fall. And then there's the man — who knows, he might be carrying an enormous knife, the one he threatened the woman with, or a gun, or he might smash your head in with a rock and kill you if you dare to intervene. You freeze, then make a run for it. You run, pushing your way through the brambles, covering your ears so you don't have to hear the woman's now clearly audible and desperate screams.

You wake with a start from this recurring nightmare, dripping with sweat and feeling terribly guilty. Sometimes you say to yourself: It's okay, it was only a dream, you don't need to feel guilty. And then you recall Jasone's voice saying 'This is a war'. She's been coming out with things like that ever since she's been part of that book club, and it makes you feel uncomfortable because you aren't entirely sure which side she sees her husband on, in which of the trenches. You don't even really know who this war is between. Are you involved too? Every time your wife uses the word 'war' you feel guilty, and it's not fair.

Jasone is adamant that all your physical complaints will disappear as soon as you finish the book and calm down.

'Success will have you back giving interviews like the Ismael Alberdi we all know, in that writerly voice...'

'Stop it, Jasone...'

'...silently staring off into the middle distance for a second before responding to each question...'

'That's enough.'

'The praise will cure you and you know it. There's nothing like a podium to restore you writers to health.'

She never used to be this snarky with you. She talks to you as if you were somehow all men — the homogeneous mass of men as she sees them. She talks to you as if you were out to get power and success at any cost — the same shit that gets thrown at men in the books she reads. It's strange, but ever since you signed the contract to publish the Spanish translation of your book she's been even more sarcastic than normal. And when you told her about the book deal, she didn't seem particularly excited.

'That's great,' she said, 'I'm guessing you've already told Jauregi?'

Your publisher, Jauregi, is always popping up here, there and everywhere, always having to give his blessing to what you do and don't do, never far from Jasone's thoughts, as if they were back in their university days, when they were practically joined at the hip. You know that they still talk, that whenever Jauregi has a book launch at the library he stops by Jasone's desk and probably invites her for a coffee. Maybe they've already discussed your novel and how long you're taking to hand over the first draft to Jasone so that she can do the first edit, as she has with all your previous books.

'Has he sent you anything yet?'

You imagine the conversation between your publisher and your wife. Between your publisher and your editor. And you feel betrayed. You feel left out of their circle. The same way you did at university, back when Jasone published stories and poems in the student magazine she ran with Jauregi. And back when a journalism student approached them with a few stories he kept squirreled away in his rucksack like hidden treasure. They looked at you that day like an intruder. Jauregi did eventually cave in and publish one of your stories. 'Only because Jasone insisted...' he told you teasingly, pointing at her. You looked at Jasone and perhaps that was the moment you fell in love with her, your sister's friend whom you'd fancied ever since you caught a glimpse of her waiting for

28

Libe in the hallway at home.

Even now you feel left out of the writers' circle. You hate being around writers. It's only ever a matter of time before someone asks that wretched question — 'So what are you working on?' — leaving you to improvise some lie that you end up believing as well. You don't enjoy writers' conversations, always turning over the same old shit, asking the same questions: 'What did you make of so-and-so's latest?' You feel like you're in the middle of a never-ending exam, under constant tension. They're not natural conversations. Writers weigh up the potential response to whatever they're about to say. They choose their words carefully, as if life were one long word game. It puts you on edge having to have your read-between-the-lines detector constantly switched on.

Jauregi also talks to you differently since you signed the contract for the Spanish translation of the novel. With a hint of resentment, jealousy, or perhaps fear that the Spanish edition might overshadow the Basque original, but always with his usual sarcasm, his 'classic Jauregi' brand of humour.

'Right, so when are we due? I would have thought you'd be having contractions by now.'

'We're getting there,' you say.

'That's a short answer for such a long gestation... You're going to have to be a bit more forthcoming when they whisk you off on a book tour round Spain.'

By now you're used to the snigger with which he ends every sentence, but you've never liked it. You've never liked Jauregi's jokey tone, just as you didn't like the way he implied that he was only publishing your story because Jasone asked him to. And you got a similar feeling years later when you were working on a novel and you asked Jasone to put you in touch with Jauregi, who, by then, had his own publishing house. On that occasion, too, you got the sense that he only agreed to read your novel because Jasone asked him to.

You didn't like him back then, but you needed him, and today you still can't stand his jokes, or how he loves to remind you that he's known Jasone for longer than you have, but you also recognise that you need him. You trust him implicitly when it comes to your writing, just as you continue to trust the editorial filter that is Jasone.

Just for a moment, you remember the time when you wrote without being a writer. In those days writing was your little secret. Hardly anyone knew anything about you or had any expectations of you: not your university friends in the very early days, not the guys from the paper where you worked after that, not even your closest friends, although you've never really had any very close friends. Back then, you wrote freely, effortlessly, imagining situations that you enjoyed resolving. You didn't have to share your secret hobby with anyone. For you, writing was like doing a sudoku by yourself, reclining in an armchair. You were perfectly happy living in that marvellous geeky universe. It was yours and yours alone. That private space smelled of burnt sugar, the smell of your mother's crème caramel in the kitchen in Eibar. Now, though, and ever since you've felt there was a public out there waiting for you, the white desk where you write has smelled of disinfectant, of cleaning products, of emptiness. Like your head.

Sometimes Vidarte appears to you, buzzing around the studio. Resting on the wall like a fly, he tells you that a writer cannot write about what he already knows, he needs to write about what he doesn't know, and that writing is the writer's way of finding that out. And you reply that every day you sit down to search for something new and unknown, something that will carry you off like a wave and wash you up on unfamiliar shores. But all you find are commonplaces.

And then you think: what am I doing talking to a fly?

Next, you wonder if it would be better simply to own up to what's happening to you. Who should you tell first… Jasone? Jauregi? Your publisher in Madrid? But something inside stops you. Some powerful force, like an undertow, refuses to let you look like a loser in the eyes of the world. All you can do is knuckle down and write a new story, a story you believe in and that's truly alive in your mind, because not even mouth-to-mouth could revive the one you're working on now.

Just this afternoon, the last word you wrote looked you in the eye and said: 'You'd better call it a day'. You sat staring at that bloody word and, realising that the only thing on the page with a pulse was the cursor, you got up and went for a pee.

4

I'll leave you to write in peace

You finished your last novel over two years ago, back when you were based in the old part of town and your daughters still lived at home. You would hear their voices and laughter in the background as you wrote. Now that they've gone, there's no more chatter or music to distract you — no more Amy Winehouse, Coldplay or Gatibu. Now it's just you and Jasone, but even Jasone spends less time at home than she used to, back when she would always be either helping the girls with their schoolwork, making supper, putting her feet up after spending the night in hospital — first with her mother, and then with her father — or working for you, making the first and final edits to your writing. She doesn't keep the bookshelves as neatly as she used to either: the classics arranged in alphabetical order (Camus, Chekhov, Duras, Faulkner, Flaubert); contemporary works arranged by publisher. She used to devote hours to organizing, re-reading and discussing books with you. But ever since you moved to the suburbs, Jasone spends less and less time at home. Now she goes out for dinner with colleagues, to the cinema with friends, or to the feminist book club. She's always busy doing something. Even when she's at home she doesn't have much time for you. She chats on the phone to the girls or to Libe, and at night she stays up late in the living room with her laptop, tying up something at work. Since her parents died, one soon after the other, and since your daughters moved out, Jasone just isn't the same. She always has something to do, somewhere to go…

'I'll leave you to write in peace…' she says, standing in front of the mirror, getting ready to go out.

She's started taking more care over her appearance, the way she used to before she had the girls. She's gone back to having a fringe. Suddenly, the old Jasone is back, the one who used to write in the student magazine, the one who never missed a gig with your sister Libe. That Jasone, not the librarian you've been married to for twenty years. Something has breathed new life into her and you don't know what it is. It's not that she looks any younger, because her face and body, grown slacker now, betray her age. Yet there's something in her gaze, a new light, that you can't quite pin down. That's why you've started going through her bag while she showers and gets changed before supper. That's why you started checking her mobile phone. You were looking for something. And today you finally found it.

When Jasone went to take a shower, you again rummaged through her rucksack. And all your searching in recent months was justified by what you found: a plastic folder containing typed pages with hand-written edits on them. Straight away you were reminded of the edits she makes to your texts. You instantly recognised that particular way of circling a word and sending it with an arrow to another part of the sentence, those notes written vertically in the margins. You only managed to read the first paragraph and then, when you heard Jasone get out of the shower, quickly put the folder back in her rucksack.

'The sound of a sliding door opening. Just describing it fills me with terror. I only have to imagine it for my heart to start pounding, for me to wet myself with fear.'

You couldn't get those three sentences out of your head all through supper. You didn't mention it to her, preferring to let her bring it up. But she didn't. She tossed the salad, served you, then herself, sipped her water. Once she'd finished eating she sat staring at the glass in front of her, twiddling her wedding ring: she often does this when she's thinking. And you've noticed that lately she's been talking less, and is somewhat absent. It's very odd that she didn't mention that text; she always tells you about what she's reading, about what she's going to propose for the next book club meeting, about the latest news from the library. Jasone definitely likes discussing literature more than you do. She always has. Until recently, the pair of you have always discussed your characters and the plots of your novels... That's why you find it so strange to think that she's begun writing again, after so long, without telling you.

Although it's also possible that the ball in your head is leading you astray. Some friend from the book club has probably asked her to read something she's written. Book clubs are full of people who would like to write. People who still dream of writing. Almost like you at the moment.

JASONE

5

The sound of a sliding door opening

I described my rape — in great detail. Not that it really happened. I described my rape in a Word document, in words that fitted seamlessly together, one after the other, as if they'd spent a long time arranging themselves inside my head. And I thought: any woman could do this. Describe her rape, I mean, even though it never happened. Because we've all lived in dread of that nightmare. We've all walked down the street with that possibility prowling around in our head. And at our backs.

My rape — should I call it my imaginary rape? — begins with the sound made by the sliding door on a transit van. I'm walking down the street at night, listening to my own footsteps, my key ring squeezed tightly in my hand, the ends of the keys sticking out between my fingers, and suddenly *rrrass*, the grating sound of a sliding door opening, the door of a white van parked by the kerb.

Like an 'abracadabra', that sound, *rrrass*, opens the mouth of the pit, and there I am, like Alice, falling down a black hole, my arms pinned behind me, my mouth covered, heading into the darkness. And in the murky pit everything happens both very quickly and very slowly. I try to turn away from the hot breath in my ear, I try to keep my trousers on by crossing my ankles, I try to clench my thighs shut... Are there two men? Or three? I don't know. I stop struggling. I let myself go limp so that it hurts less, so that they'll leave me alone as soon as possible, like a soldier in a battle pretending to be dead. I've always thought that if I was ever in a battle, I would pretend to be dead. I am a dead body on a battlefield.

A sliding door. A sliding door only has to open for me to go from hearing a man saying 'Hi, gorgeous' in the last bar I was in, standing there under the neon lights, to hearing another — or is it the same man? — whispering 'you slut' in my ear, inside a van, among piles of cardboard and toolboxes. A sliding door only has to open for the coach to turn into a pumpkin. For the glass slipper to shatter.

Rrrass. The sound of a sliding door opening. Just describing it fills me with terror. I only have to imagine it for my heart to start pounding, for me to wet myself with fear.

I don't know what drove me to write about it, to describe my imaginary rape. Or, rather, I don't know why I didn't do it sooner, why I didn't set it down on paper before, because I realise now that it has always been there, in my bones, under my skin, and yet invisible to my eyes. Like all the most basic things. Perhaps what woke up all my demons was the thought that my daughter Eider had been in Pamplona the same night the gang-rape took place. Perhaps the shock only dredged up what I've been carrying inside me all these years. Ever since my girlfriends and I started going out at night on our own, or probably before that.

'Let's go back along the main road, Jaso,' Libe would say.

'It's better lit.'

It always seemed perfectly normal to us to draw up a strategy for getting home at night. Libe and I would leave the last bar in the old part of town and walk together to some mutually convenient spot. Then we'd say goodbye and head for our respective homes almost holding our breath. I never ran, I just walked very fast. I was afraid to run. I was afraid to show I was afraid. I didn't want to think about my trembling body, or my face, white with fear.

We had strategies for every situation. Like walking more slowly if we felt someone was following us.

'Slow right down and see if he overtakes you. If he doesn't, then run,' Libe would say. She was always more clued-up about these things than me. 'Or look in a window and wave, so he thinks someone's expecting you. And if things turn ugly, you know what to do, knee him in the balls and run.'

The number of men we must have kneed in the balls in our dreams.

I described my rape and I thought: the only reason we didn't get raped more often was because we were good strategists. We didn't get assaulted more often because whenever we passed a group of men at night, we would always look down, avoid their eyes and walk past as quickly as possible or else cross the road. We didn't get groped more often because we didn't go to those late-night bars, those woman-traps, even though we wanted to keep partying. Worse things didn't happen to us because we were brought up to be afraid and our fear had protected us. Yes, our fear was our defence.

I described my rape and I thought: good God, this must have come from somewhere deep inside me. And it exploded, like a firecracker on New Year's Eve. When I re-read it, I was surprised by the details, the sounds, the smells... They were all there inside me. I thought: I've kept a rape locked inside me all these years, and I only realised how much space it was taking up when it came out as words on the page.

Describing my rape woke up a part of me I thought lay dormant, lost: it meant my return to writing stories after a very long time. Once I'd written that scene, I couldn't stop writing. I sat in the dining room with my laptop each night, not telling Ismael what I was really doing. I said I had some work things to finish, or that I had to prepare for the next book club meeting; and so, in secret, I started telling a story that began with a woman describing her rape. And once the cork was out of the bottle, everything else spilled out too, everything that woman had kept inside her, ready to explode one day. What exploded was her story of silence and submission and, without my realising it, so did my story, our story. And I say 'our story' because behind her every word I seemed to hear the echo of many other voices. For the first time, I felt that, stored away in my body, were the bodies of other women. That their bodies had always been there inside mine, whispering advice on how to take the next step. *If* I should take it.

Describing my rape meant my return to telling stories, my return to the days when I used to write. Back then, I was always eager to finish writing a story so that I could show it to Jauregi and have it published in the magazine, or to Libe, my best friend and my most enthusiastic reader. This time, however, I didn't show it to anyone. Certainly not to Ismael. I didn't dare tell my husband I had gone back to writing. And I thought: at some point I'll have to tell him, so as to rid myself of this guilt about writing in secret. But I didn't know how he would take it. After all, I told myself, he's the writer in this house. Ismael Alberdi. I'm just the wife who edits what he writes before he sends it off to Jauregi at the publishing house.

6

I'm here, had you forgotten about me?

I kept my novel secret, just as, for years, I'd kept the scene of that imaginary rape secreted away in my subconscious. Often, when Ismael went off to bed, I would sit up late writing. Sometimes I wondered if Ismael even remembered that I used to write, and long before he began writing too. Perhaps I should have just casually reminded him. There was no reason to keep it a secret, but somehow I needed to, for reasons I still couldn't put into words. I might not have the words, but I did have a body with a memory, which was telling me I should conceal my return to writing, or even forget about it altogether. This was what those insistent women's voices were whispering in my ear.

Besides, I didn't know how to bring the subject up, how to explain that the door to writing had reopened, and what it had revealed was nothing less than my own rape. He just won't understand, I thought. How could I convince him of the truth contained in the words I'd written, how could I tell him that the stories born inside us are often more real than the ones that occur in the outside world. And how could I explain something like that to a writer of all people, to someone who should know this better than anyone.

'How can you describe your rape if you've never been raped?'

I imagined him asking me something like that, and in the subtext I read: 'How can you write if you aren't even a writer?'

No, I wasn't a writer. I didn't tackle the major themes of the world. 'Not bad,' he used to say whenever he read one of my stories, in the days before we were married. He always considered my themes to be minor themes. To him, my words didn't smell of the ink of the great classics, didn't have the giddy pace of great adventure stories. To him, my words smelled of cupcakes and lip balm.

And so I kept bumping up against a wall that prevented me from telling him anything. Perhaps that wall was the result of me having internalised the idea that Ismael is the only writer in the household. And I was merely the keen-eyed editor who noticed what he didn't. The complement to his work and his success.

'You "new Basques" are very good at that kind of thing,' he told me the first time he asked for my help with his debut novel, and I know he didn't just seek my opinion because Basque is my second language, one that I had actually learned and studied (and which apparently means I'm quicker to spot any grammatical errors); he's always sought my seal of approval before sending off his typescripts to Jauregi. He knows that when it comes to literature, Jauregi and I have similar tastes, having spent our university years together discussing books, organising readings, and choosing stories and poems for the student magazine we edited. He doesn't want to disappoint

Jauregi. He couldn't bear to disappoint him even with a first draft. In fact, he can't bear to disappoint anyone. And he's always found my opinion and my suggestions helpful and reassuring.

Having said that, he does also regularly trot out that stuff about how I have a clearer vision of Basque because I learned it as a second language: 'You "new Basques"', he says and I don't know why he doesn't simply say 'You "pseudo-Basques"'. He doesn't realise it, but every time he calls me a new Basque, my mind goes back to the image of the 'me' I've kept hidden away ever since secondary school, the 'me' who appears in the photo of my First Communion, alongside the family who travelled up to the Basque Country from Zamora for that special day: Granny, Grandad and the uncle who lived with us. The entire clan. Then there's that name written on my First Communion name card: Asunción. The name that has always given me such a complex.

'Does he live with you?' Libe asked me once on seeing my uncle leaving our apartment. 'Doesn't he have his own place?'

'It's only temporary… Until they tell him he can definitely carry on working at the factory,' I replied, unable to hide my embarrassment.

Having my uncle still living with us made us poorer. It made our home and family poorer. It made us more immigrant, more Spanish, even though we weren't nationalistic flag-wavers. The only flags we flew were my father's and uncle's work overalls hung out to dry on the balcony.

The first time I met Libe at university I told her my name was Jasone. Her family had moved from Eibar in the north of the country where her father had worked in a factory whose owner had decided to relocate to Vitoria, as a lot of other industrialists were doing at the time. That was the moment I buried Asunción, my name up until then. I rebaptised myself. With my new, translated name I felt I'd also shrugged off all the Spanish words and names that had stuck to me like tar ever since I was born: *yaya, yayo, tío, mamá, papá*. Libe, another newcomer to Vitoria, was my chance to be someone else. To be like her. My father worked in a factory, so did hers. Deep down we weren't so very different, even if to me it felt as if her father had brought an entire factory with him from Eibar, while mine had come emptyhanded. As if her father had arrived having already made his name, whereas mine, an unskilled labourer, had come with no name or surname at all.

I only got to know Ismael later on. We'd coincided at a few events, but we didn't really speak until Libe's arrest.

When I arrived at his parents' house on that terrible morning, he said: 'Thanks for your help with my story,' meaning the story of his that we'd included in the magazine. He seemed very young back then. Libe's little brother. I only had eyes for the older boys, for Jauregi mostly, and for the guys he hung out with at demonstrations and gigs... But that would also change.

Things do change.

Things can always change.

So I kept my novel to myself just as I did my rape. And in the meantime, I waited for Ismael to bring me his novel, as he had done with all the others, but it never came, even though I knew the deadline was looming.

'Hasn't he shown you anything yet?' Jauregi would

sometimes ask.

No, I would tell him, this time Ismael hadn't even wanted to show me an early draft, and I was still waiting. I was waiting, too, for Jauregi to stop talking about my husband, because whenever he did, I felt as if my husband were a piece of meat that had got stuck between my teeth. I was waiting for him to talk to me as his fellow student at university, the woman he'd always viewed slightly differently, the woman he was constantly joking with and teasing, which was his way of getting closer to the people who really interested him. There was always something, though, a permanent tension, like a taut cord that never snapped, because of the situation, the atmosphere, the fear. There was a physical tension between us, but also an intellectual one. However, once he started publishing Ismael's work, he stopped talking to me, to Jasone, and began talking to Ismael's wife. The cord slackened. Suddenly, he made me feel as if I smelled of cupcakes and air freshener. And although, for a while, I resigned myself to this, the moment he reminded me that I was also a writer, I suddenly felt the need to recover the old Jasone I used to see reflected in his eyes. I felt my whole body calling out, releasing a scream I'd kept locked up inside for a long time:

'Hey, I'm here, had you forgotten about me?'

When I described my imaginary rape, a lot of buried memories rose to the surface. I remembered, for example, that when I was very young, my early sexual fantasies all resembled rapes. They lacked the violence of a real rape, but the sex was definitely nonconsensual. I'd be in my bikini on a lilo in a private swimming pool, with my hands tied, and a handsome man would be touching my nipples with his fingers, then he would reach under my bikini top and cover my whole breast with his hand. And I would be saying No, No, but deep down I wanted to say Yes, Yes. And then he would slide his hand down inside my bikini bottom and I would still be saying No, all the while arching my back with pleasure. Over the years, I've come to realise that the reason I dreamed such things was because this was the only way I could enjoy sex without feeling guilty, without feeling afraid I was doing something I shouldn't be doing. Or perhaps, too, because, ever since I was a child, I had so internalised the idea that abuse was something normal, even sexy, that I ended up unconsciously including it in my desires. And while I was writing, a part of my past I had thought lost suddenly reappeared. It was while writing that I began to understand what lay behind my thinking, because there's always a reason.

Perhaps that's why it's dangerous to write. It's like a dangerous low tide that reveals the rocks hidden beneath the water. And we don't always like what appears, because then the words we use while bobbing safely about on the surface all disappear, the words that survive like a lilo adrift on the waters all vanish; and other words appear, the ones that weigh like lead, the ones that live on the seabed and can only be seen when the tide goes out. And along with those words appear bits of plastic, Tetra-pak cartons, rusty Coca-Cola cans, a shotgun cartridge, a panty liner all bloated like the body of a drowned man. We don't always like what appears when we write.

In my words I found a long-suppressed pain I hadn't really been aware of. When I read what I'd written, I felt as if my body had been subjected to a prolonged beating, as if, for years, someone had been raping me while I was drugged, anaesthetised. I couldn't remember what had happened. I could only feel the pain. A distilled pain. A depilated pain. I wouldn't have been able to explain it to a judge. I had no proof. Pain isn't proof. I would lose my case. Perhaps that's why I started writing again. Because I needed proof. Evidence.

And little by little it began to appear.

ISMAEL

7

This is a war

Since the girls left home, you rarely turn on the television after supper. It used to be an excuse for us to all come together at the end of the day and talk. The family gathered around the fire. These days you and Jasone have supper together then go straight to bed to read. Although, more recently, over the past year, Jasone will stay up in the living room at her laptop and come to bed later. Since you found those typed pages in her rucksack, you suspect that perhaps she's been editing them. Yesterday you went through her bag again, but it was no longer there. It left you wanting to read more.

Tonight she's in bed, reading. She turned in before you did. You watch her from the bathroom. She seems somehow distant.

When you walk over to her, Jasone glances up from her book, pulls her glasses down onto the tip of her nose and mentions your daughter Maialen's visit with her boyfriend on the weekend just gone.

'Do you think Maialen's happy with that boy?'

Jasone always brings up the deep stuff when you've barely

got enough neurons left to put on your pyjamas.

'I guess so,' you reply, undressing.

'You don't like him, do you?'

'You mean *you* don't like him. I was polite enough, wasn't I?' You lift up the sheets and stand there for a moment, as if wondering whether or not to get in. 'I wasn't too disapproving, was I?'

'Ismael, the look on your face said: "So you're the one fucking my daughter."'

'That's enough, Jaso...'

Your wife would never have come out with something like that before. You don't know what's come over her.

'Oh, *I've* gone too far! It's different, then, when the woman we're talking about is your daughter... By the way, Eider is going to Turkey with a friend.'

'To Turkey? And no one thought to tell me?'

'I'm telling you now... And, relax, she's not a little girl anymore. She doesn't need our protection.'

'Or our permission, I suppose.'

You think back to the day you gave Eider permission to go to Pamplona. Now they don't need your blessing for anything. No one asks you anything anymore. You're not even sure what your place in the family is anymore. You have no authority over anyone now. Not your daughters. And not Jasone.

Jasone goes back to her book and after reading a few lines she looks up again as if to say something. You wait for her to make some comment on the book she's reading, as she usually does. A lot of the time, especially when she's reading something for her book club, she'll tell you the name of the author, always a woman, and you won't dare tell her you've never heard of her. You don't want to open up the same old argument: about how you don't know what women are writing about now, how you don't value women's writing… You're bored with the whole business of calling everything into question. It's Libe's influence, it's Jasone repeating what she reads in the books Libe recommends to her. Setting up the book club at the library was also Libe's idea. But try telling any of this to Jasone without her going ballistic.

'I can't get what happened to that girl out of my head,' she tells you. 'The one they found up in the hills.'

Your breathing suddenly quickens. Jasone has touched a nerve, the one that, for some unknown reason, you find so discomfiting.

'Me neither. I don't know what the world's coming to,' you reply.

'What it's coming to?' she asks, raising her eyebrows and slipping her bookmark into her book. A clear sign she's gearing up for an argument. 'You say that like it was something new.'

'No, but… Ever since what happened in Pamplona, it's like it's the only topic…'

You reply a little fearfully, as if weighing each word. You know you can't joke with Jasone about this. You know what she's going to say next, she's going to say that this is a war. She probably got that from Libe too.

'This is a war, Isma. And it didn't start yesterday. It's the longest war in history.'

You're tempted to tell her not to conflate two separate issues, that what happened is awful, that only a monster would be capable of doing that to a girl, but that it was a case of rape and murder, not a war. You're tempted to say that the girl wasn't raped and murdered by all the men in the world, that not all men are the same, that the only thing those sorts of slogans achieve is to make you feel guilty, and make men defensive. But you don't say anything. You don't say any of that. There's no reasoning with her. She didn't used to be like this.

'This is a war, Isma, can't you see?' she repeats, raising her voice now. Spoiling for a fight, you think.

It's all those books Libe sends her. They put ideas in her head. And that bloody book club. But it's also because she's worried. Even if she won't admit it, even if she tells you a hundred times that your daughters can look after themselves, Jasone is also scared for them.

'Relax, Jasone.'

'Relax? That's precisely the problem. I don't know how you men can be so relaxed…'

'Who says I'm relaxed? And don't pigeonhole me. If you must know, I'm having nightmares about what happened to that girl, that's how relaxed I am,' you blurt out. 'It scares me too. It sickens me.'

'Nightmares? What about? Being raped?'

'No. I keep dreaming about a girl being beaten up and raped.'

'But you've never had the feeling you are that woman?'

'Well, no.'

Jasone falls silent for a moment.

'You've never got inside a woman's skin, not even in your dreams?'

You're entering dangerous territory. You know you're about to say something you shouldn't say.

'No, actually, I don't think I have. Should I feel guilty about that as well?... And what's that look supposed to mean? I suppose you regularly dream that you're a man.'

'I don't know if I dream I'm a man, but I've often got inside a man's skin...' Jasone points to the books on the shelf. 'Every time I read, for example. I'm Carlos, David... I'm Gregor Samsa. I get inside the characters' skin without even thinking about the fact that they're men, without even thinking about the fact that I am not a man. It seems you men find it harder to do the same.'

You feel like telling her that maybe it's because women never let us in to their secret world, that inaccessible space... How can you men get inside a woman's skin if you don't really know what women are like? If you don't know any of their secrets, not even your partner's secrets?

Jasone is silent for a moment before continuing her point.

'I've no doubt at all that what happened to that girl deeply hurts you men, but at the same time you have to acknowledge that it isn't your pain. It's a pain and fear you feel for your daughters, your partners, your sisters... The pain you *would* feel were something like that to happen to them. But it's not really yours.'

'Jasone... Please, stop pigeonholing me. Stop saying "you men". I'm me. Not all men.'

Every time Jasone says 'you men', you feel guilty. And even though you'd rather not recognise yourself as part of any group, the proof is there, just beneath the epidermis, like an internal tattoo: the image of you and your father going off to hunt back when you lived in Eibar, and the image of your mother and Libe doing the grocery shopping. Two worlds.

Two groups. Two teams. Them the women, and you the men. When Libe told your father she wanted to go out looking for Aitor with you both, he wouldn't let her.

'No, we'll go,' he told her. 'You two stay at home.'

We the men, and them the women.

And included in that 'them' are your daughters. The fear you feel for them. What are you afraid of? Of men like you? Or of *other* men? Where are they lurking? In which cave? Are they in Turkey? In Pamplona? Or sharing an apartment with your daughters? Are they their friends? Their boyfriends? Who is that man raping the woman in your dreams? You're nothing like him. That 'you' they try to apply to all men is unfair.

You can't stand your wife's know-it-all tone when she talks about men and women, that way of speaking to you as if you were mentally impaired, as if you didn't understand anything. What does she mean you're not capable of getting inside a woman's skin? You're a writer! You can get inside anyone's skin. You think about the woman who appears in your nightmare, and you imagine writing about her. In fact, you feel a sudden urge to write about her. To hear her voice. Perhaps that's the way to finally scare off your ghosts.

'And what if the main character of my novel were a woman?' you hear yourself say.

'A woman? Really?'

'What? Don't you think I could?'

'Of course you could… But, just be careful: getting inside our skin isn't the same as putting words in our mouths.'

'Oh, give me strength…' You press your hand to your forehead, as if you were feeling feverish.

'Don't do that.'

'How exactly do you expect me to write about someone else if not by putting words in their mouth?'

'Maybe the only way to write from her perspective is to find something of yourself in there, something you share in common with her. Something that's inside both of you. And to do that you're going to have to look her squarely in the eye.'

You don't say anything, and wait for Jasone to offload onto you all the theory she's been accumulating from all her enlightening reading.

'Have you at any moment asked yourself from what position you're observing this woman? The position from which you men look at us women?'

'What are you talking about? Stop talking about me in the plural. I've told you: I'm me. Just me.'

'Yes, you're you, but you can't deny there's also a "we", a "we" that learns from a young age what it means to be a man.'

'I think I'm still working that out…'

'Well, it basically consists in having to demonstrate on a daily basis that you're not a woman… Or a poof either, of course.'

'Jaso, what is going on with you? I don't do either of those things.'

'Oh, really? You should hear yourself talking to your father. You should hear the manly voice you put on when you speak to him…'

This is a low blow. She has no right to say that to you. Why's she bringing up your father now?

'I think we'd better drop it,' you reply, feeling offended. You lie down on your back, and switch off your bedside lamp.

Jasone places her book on her bedside table, turns off her

57

light and curls up, her back to you, without saying another word.

You lie there awake for some time, staring up at the ceiling. What voice is she talking about? What voice do you use when you're with your father? Isn't it the same voice you use with everyone? You close your eyes and hear your father's deep baritone singing somewhere in the distance; singing the hymn of Saint Ignatius of Loyola, the patron saint of Guipúzcoa and Vizcaya, which he taught you when you were a boy: «Inaxio, *gure patroi handixa...*». And you're singing along with him, imitating that fine, manly voice. The voice of a real man.

8

The good old songs

Now, from up on the top of the hill, you confirm something
you've always suspected. Everything would have turned out
better if Libe, your sister, had joined the search party for Aitor
instead of you. If Libe had done many of the things you were
made to do. But your father was adamant that it wasn't right.
Just as it wasn't right for you to sing those songs with your
sister. Libe must have been sixteen, you thirteen. The two of
you would put the Itoiz cassette in the player in Libe's room
and start singing: *'Eremuko dunen atzetik dabil, zulo urdin
guztiak miatu ezinik, eta euri zitalari esker bizi da...'.* You
remember singing along as you helped your sister write the
names of the bands she taped on the cassette covers. But the
days of singing together eventually came to an end; as you
grew older, you each came to occupy your own space. Two
worlds.

One Christmas around that time, your parents bought you
an upright piano. Your father decided that if his son was so
very fond of singing, he should at least sing proper songs, the
good old songs, which he would teach the boy himself, and not

the songs he learned with his sister. 'The good old songs. The songs we always sang,' your father would say emphasising the 'we'. You can still remember your father pressing down the keys with his two forefingers, with their square fingernails, and singing: *'I-na-xio gu-re pa-troi han-di-xa...'*

Once you had learned 'the good old songs', a part of you began to die, something spread slowly through you like an antibiotic, gradually killing any desire to sing with your sister Libe. Perhaps that was the moment when your two worlds, your places in the world, began to split apart. From then on, Libe was the only one who sang at home. Initially, songs by Silvio Rodríguez and Pablo Milanés, then by Dire Straits, and soon enough bands like Kortatu, Tijuana in Blue and RIP would enter her life with words like: 'In love with death...', as well as radical Basque rock groups like Korroskada, Cicatriz and Hertzainak: 'Kill Dad, kill him...' And with them, the dark atmosphere of political militancy. La Polla and Barricada: 'Someone has to pull the trigger...' It was then that Libe's door closed to you for good. And it's never reopened.

Ever since then, your sister has always skittered away from you like a lizard, she's never let you in on her feelings, on who she really is. How then is one supposed to understand women? Not that you made much of an effort to enter that cave. A dark and dangerous cave. It always frightened you to see your sister on the militant frontline. You knew from the start there would be consequences. Libe was arrested by the Civil Guard and spent five days in solitary confinement, imprisoned under the antiterrorism act. You've never spoken to her about what happened, or what she went through during those five days. By then, there were already many miles separating you, and that was before she moved to Berlin. She was eventually released without charge.

Libe would have done a better job than you are writing a novel about the oppressive political atmosphere of those years. Yes, that's another thing she would have done better than you. You always steered well clear of all of that. Your only real involvement in the conflict was Libe's arrest and the time you were asked to deliver a package to Vitoria. You just had to drop it off at a bar in the city, as your cousin Aitor asked you to do the day you went back to Eibar for a hunting trip with your father. You didn't know what it contained. You didn't dare ask him anything. The look in Aitor's eyes didn't allow for any questions. You took the parcel, put it in your bag, and when your father told you that you'd be going back to Vitoria without him, on the bus, that he was going to stay in Eibar to have dinner at the hunting club with his uncle and their friends, you suddenly felt so alone, so afraid, you could have sworn the parcel was pulsating, that it had a life of its own. When you got onto the bus, you slipped it under your seat. You spent the entire journey imagining that parcel was about to explode and blow you and your fellow passengers to smithereens, and that chunks of you all would go flying through the air, exactly as happened to those two ETA guys whose bomb blew up in their faces. You were so terrified by the time you reached the bus station in Vitoria that you couldn't bring yourself to pick up the parcel. You left it there, and with it your one chance to become a hero, your one chance ever to have a song or graffiti penned in your honour, your one chance to not be an official coward. And your fear grew whenever you saw your cousin or anyone else caught up in the violent atmosphere in which your sister lived.

An atmosphere you've been trying to revisit in your new novel. But you've been deluding yourself if you thought you could write something credible about the conflict. How could you, if, unlike your sister, you never saw the inside of a police station, if you never spent a single sleepless night thinking that the Civil Guard was going to arrive in the small hours and break down the front door, if you never had to check under your car before turning on the ignition to make sure a bomb wasn't going to blow you to bits? How can you write about a conflict you only observed from a safe distance? Like those journalists who write articles about wars without ever leaving their hotel rooms. Everything you've written up to now reads like it's made out of cardboard. It rings false. The words have no heart. How can you describe suffering if you don't put your heart into every word?

And now, from up on top of the hill, you ask yourself what's really making your heart beat faster. It must be that other 'war', to use Jasone's word, that nightmare about the woman being beaten and raped up in the hills that's dragging you out of your comfort zone. Just seeing it in your mind's eye makes you feel like you can't breathe. That mixture of fear and guilt, that deep well of black thoughts. Why do you feel so terrible? The truth is, you don't know. It's something as yet undiscovered. It's as if, behind the image of the woman being raped, there were other hidden stories pulsating beneath the very ground you tread. But what stories? And why are they pursuing you?

Vidarte re-enters your mind. Resting on the wall of your study like a fly, he reminds you that a writer shouldn't write about what he already knows, but about what he doesn't know, and doesn't want to discover. Writing is the writer's way of discovering that. And why not? Perhaps this is his last chance. Perhaps what you talked about with Jasone was really a premonition.

'Should I write about that woman? About that stranger?' you ask the fly on the wall.

While you wait for an answer you think about how absurd it is to think that you're going to find it harder to get inside a woman's skin, as Jasone implied you would. You're a writer and can get inside anyone's skin. Of course you can. And you're going to give it a go. Even if time is running out.

9

You could take Dad home with you

You sit down in your study, in front of the computer screen, with the enthusiasm of someone about to write the first line of a story. There's always plenty of enthusiasm in the first line, plenty of open ground. The doors start to close as you write, marking out a set path. To write is to lose a little more freedom with each paragraph. But in the first line, you're free. You're not dependent on anyone. You're not yet a slave to your own words. The same thing happens in life: the options become scarcer as you move through it.

You want to get closer to this woman, to find out what she thinks, what she feels. But you aren't quite sure where to start. You have conflicting feelings about her. You want to see her as if she were you, but you can't stop your own sense of guilt from casting a shadow over her, your shadow, preventing you from really seeing her. You hate to have to say this, but last night in bed Jasone posed exactly the right question, the one you can't seem to answer: from what position are you observing this woman? You just don't know. She told you that men find it harder to see women because it's harder to see what's in the margins, unilluminated, in the shadows. You have to make a real effort to see it, she said. And while Jasone's words come back to you, while you strain to see those margins you know nothing about, just then, your mobile phone starts to vibrate. It's a long number, one you don't recognise.

At first, when the person at the other end of the line tells you they're calling from the hospital, you think it must be about the tumour in your brain. An urgent call from the hospital to have you admitted and operated on as soon as possible. They've finally worked out that there really is a black ball inside your head which is preventing you from thinking clearly. The idea that they're about to tell you that you have a tumour fills you with a strange and appalling sense of satisfaction. No more pressure, no more deadlines, no more feeling guilty that you have nothing more to offer. At last you have a justification for your failure. But no. The call is about your mother. She fainted in the street and broke her hip.

You race to the hospital, where you find your mother on the emergency ward with one cheek all swollen and grazed, and one arm lying motionless on top of the sheets to keep the intravenous drip from becoming detached. She's wearing a hospital wristband bearing her name and details. It reminds you of the ones they put on your daughters' wrists when they were born.

She looks like she's been beaten up.

You go over to her, but you're not sure what to do: whether to take her hand in yours; whether to lean over and give her a kiss, hug her. You find yourself incapable of doing anything. But then, nobody ever showed you how to do those things in that kitchen with its white floor tiles, with its hot dinners and cold conversations. Nobody ever showed you when is the right moment for a hug, or how to give it, or what you're supposed to do with your body when you receive one. Your mother didn't give you much time to think. She threw you out of there before you'd even opened your mouth.

'Thank goodness you're here. You must go home right away,' she says, the second you reach her side.

'Hold on, how are you?'

She tries to play down her condition, even though she's wincing in pain. She's been well trained.

'Fine. I'm being looked after here... Go to your father. You know he doesn't like being on his own. And call Libe.'

Your mother is worried about her husband. Ever since his memory started to go, she's avoided leaving him at home for long periods of time. Although she didn't really do that even before then. In recent years she's used your father's health as her excuse for not going out; before that, she stayed at home without the need for any excuse. Especially once your father retired. After that, her mornings of blithely running errands were over. After that, she was always in a hurry to get home. Where have you been? Afraid of being late.

It's strange to see your mother lying on a bed, not moving, suddenly vulnerable, unable to accept that she can't run the show as she always has. Seeing her like this it's hard to believe she's the same woman who would stand in the kitchen plucking the quails her husband had shot before moving on to dice the onions for the Espagnole sauce that went with them. The same woman who would rummage around in that old biscuit tin full of buttons of all sizes and colours, to sew one onto a shirt, jacket or jumper. The woman who would put aside money in that tin in order to one day buy herself a faux fur coat to wear to Sunday mass. The same one who would knit you scarves that itched like mad. 'What do you mean they're itchy? You are a sensitive bunch.' The same one who continued to knit scarves to send to Libe in Berlin. 'It gets very cold over there.'

But now your mother is another person entirely. Someone who needs protection, care. Until today you'd never seen her like this. You'd never seen her with such small, needy eyes.

Just as you're leaving the emergency department — first shooting an apologetic glance at the nurses, as if to apologise for leaving so soon — Jasone arrives.

'Let's see if you have any more luck than I did. She threw me out,' you say with a shrug, at the same time thinking how Jasone always shows up at the right moment. 'Do you have Libe's mobile number?'

'You don't have your own sister's phone number? I'll call her now, that way I can say hello too.'

You watch her as she calls Libe, leaning against the wall in the emergency department. Jasone's eyes light up when she's talking to your big sister, her best friend. You can see the dimples appear on her cheeks before she even starts talking, even while she's listening to the dial tone. Just knowing that she's about to talk to Libe puts a smile on her face. Libe has lived in Berlin for almost twenty years, but they've never lost touch or their childhood friendship and they speak at least once a month. They also write to one another, send text messages, recommend books. When Jasone speaks to Libe it's in her old voice. A voice that's brilliant, vibrant, alive.

You've hardly spoken to your sister since she moved to Berlin. You hear about her from Jasone and your mother. Your mother likes to tell you about the NGO where Libe has worked for over a decade and where, it seems, she takes on more and more responsibilities. She's no longer out in the camps, but in the office, managing and organizing operations. Right now, according to your mother's most recent update, she's very busy setting up refugee camps in Lesbos.

The last time you saw your sister was at Christmas. She came alone, as she always does, despite having had a girlfriend in Berlin for years. She never brings her with her, never talks about her at home. That's because of your father. Everyone but your father knows Libe has a girlfriend called Kristin. One Christmas Eve supper, your father said something about her ending up single — he used the term 'spinster' — and the whole table fell silent. You wouldn't want to end up like your father, being the only one at the table not knowing what everyone else knows. There's plenty that goes unsaid in your house. Or that's spoken about on the phone when you're not around to hear it.

Libe's voice sounds tinny, but that doesn't surprise you. By the time you'd both grown up there was something cold and metallic between you. Ever since Libe began shutting her bedroom door and getting caught up in politics — something that always terrified you — and especially after her arrest, it's as if you've only ever spoken via a telephone line, even when you're right in front of each other. So it doesn't strike you as odd. The times when you would get into Libe's warm bed, when you'd play and sing together are long gone, even if that voice is the same one that would sing along with you to Itoiz's songs.

As you tell your sister what's happened to your mother,

you can't help noticing her lack of surprise, as if she'd been expecting this to happen at any moment.

'She's had this problem with her head for a while... She was waiting for the results of a scan.'

'I didn't know anything about that.'

'I think she didn't want to alarm either of you.'

You don't understand why your mother didn't tell you when you've been seeing each other every week. Or why she told her daughter who lives hundreds of miles away. Or why she said nothing to your father. Though perhaps you can understand that, given your father's current mental state, and because he's never been particularly open to hearing about other people's problems. Still, you can't imagine how you'd feel if Jasone were ill and she didn't tell you, the man with whom she's spent half her life.

Lately, you've had the sneaking feeling that the men in your family are missing out on something. That all around you there's a secret territory, a strange world, that you men have never visited. Your father is still in the dark about Libe's homosexuality, he still doesn't know his wife has been having dizzy spells for nearly a year. Libe and your wife are in contact, they regularly chat about the world's injustices, books, films... But Libe never recommends books to you, the two of you never chat... Aren't you her brother? Aren't you the writer in the family? You're starting to suspect that you're missing out on as much of the family goings-on as your father, that they're keeping things from you, that they don't tell you everything. Your daughters included. They certainly tell their mother everything. They speak to her every day, and at the end of their conversations Jasone will sometimes pass you the phone so you can say hi to them. When you take the phone, the earpiece is warm and your daughters no longer feel like talking. Everything they had to say, they've already said to their mother.

'What about Dad? Is he on his own?' Libe asks you.

'Yes.'

'Go and be with him. Go on, get over there.'

'Oh, not you as well! What's the rush? Dad's fine on his own.'

'No, he's not.'

'He's not a child...'

'He gets scared. He's scared of being on his own. Look, Isma, I can't come right now, I have a couple of important matters to tie up here, but I'll try to get some leave to come within a month. In the meantime, we have to make arrangements... And you're going to have to keep Dad company. I can arrange for Nancy to cover the mornings, but in the afternoons...'

'I have to write, I can't spend every afternoon at Dad's place.'

'You could take him home with you. Until Mum's discharged that is. You carry on working in your study and leave him sitting happily in front of the television.'

She's used to making decisions in emergencies. She's used to telling people what to do, to organising an urgent response in a crisis. But this is a different kind of crisis.

Take your father home with you. What a great idea. As if you didn't have enough problems concentrating. That's all you need, your father at home with the TV on full blast, watching afternoon gameshows, one after the other, and adverts for denture fixatives and cholesterol-lowering yogurt drinks. Your father asking you for coffee and biscuits. Your father having one of his coughing fits and almost choking. Spitting into a handkerchief and looking at what he's brought up, before folding it away and putting it back in his dressing gown pocket.

You can't take it. The image of your father with you at home is the last straw. You walk away from Jasone towards the area where the ambulances are parked. You're about to tell your sister something you haven't told anyone, as if you'd slipped back in time into that atmosphere of complicity when, terrified, you would climb into Libe's bed. You're afraid again, you're back in your sister's bed.

'Look, Libe. I have a deadline for the new novel that I'm not going to be able to meet.'

'Just tell them what's going on.'

'You don't understand, Libe. If I have Dad at home with me it's only going to make matters worse.'

Libe takes her time responding.

'Isma, I'm only asking you for a little of your time. Right now I can't come, I'm needed here. I'm really sorry to hear about the deadline and everything, but right now we need to separate out what's urgent from what's important. I spend every day doing that, in every decision I make, often with lives at stake. What's important right now are our parents, but so are the lives of many people who depend on my decisions. I'll come as soon as I can, I promise... Please take him home with you in the afternoons.'

You don't respond, but you're furious because you feel this isn't your job. You feel you're doing your sister a favour. Beneath the epidermis, branded onto you is the detail that Libe was the one who always went with your mother to do the shopping, while you went hunting with your father. Libe was the one who helped your mother make lunch, while you played football outside on the empty bit of waste ground the local boys used as a pitch. When your cousin went missing in the hills, Libe stayed at home while you accompanied your father. It's not your job now to look after him.

And besides, where have they got this idea your father is afraid? What nonsense. They talk as if they didn't know him. It shows they've never watched him in action, bounding down the most perilous hillsides like a mountain goat, not even holding on to the rocks or shrubs. He was always the first of the group to arrive. And he'd wait at the bottom, hands on hips, watching the rest of us scramble down, shouting 'Come on, we don't have all day!'

10

The best lies are also the briefest

Everything is clearer from up above. The sounds you can hear at the top of Olarizu — the crickets, the birds — and that smell of the south wind have unsurprisingly reminded you of all the hours you've spent in the hills with your father, Aitor and your uncle. The south wind was a sign that the pigeons might fly over. For your father, Aitor and your uncle — for those who knew how to hunt — the south wind was pure gold. They would stare up at the sky, still and silent among the brambles or in position up a tree, waiting for the pigeons to fly by. You would look up at the sky and then at those men, unable to understand their appetite for hunting. That silence was like the silence in your house, the suppers of hot soup and cold conversations in your white-tiled kitchen. Your father would stand like a statue, looking up at the sky, with Txo, his dog, at his side. Every now and then, they would look at each other. The man at the dog, the dog at the man. And that's when you felt out of place. Next to you would be Mendi, the other dog you kept out in the garden and that your father didn't so much as look at. Sometimes he'd say: 'We'll have to see what to do with him. He's a needless expense.' And Mendi would look up at him devotedly, with that brown patch on his left eye, aware that, for once, his master was addressing him. Whenever your father caught you stroking Mendi he'd say 'Don't stroke him, it makes dogs soft… Leave him…' You were the only one who paid any attention to Mendi, and he returned your loyalty and followed you everywhere.

'What are you doing? Don't shoot! Can't you ever wait? Look, you've scared them off now!'

On more than one occasion your father shouted at you for being overhasty and firing too soon, when the pigeons weren't yet directly overhead. He'd be furious. But you were so desperate to be the first to kill a pigeon, or at least to hit one before your cousin Aitor did. You were tired of him always being the one who had something to show when you came down from the hills and returned to town; tired of hearing your father praise your cousin's skills with the shotgun, his 'appetite for hunting'; tired of Aitor mocking you: 'No luck today either, eh, cuz?' He didn't even call you by your name.

On many occasions you hoped the south wind wouldn't blow and that the pigeons would pass by too high. You had no desire to join in that competition. But, inevitably, the south wind would return, making the pigeons fly lower. And on those days, what for the others was pure gold, was for you as cold and hard as the metal barrel of your shotgun. You thought going to live in Vitoria would remove you from that world, but you and your father kept returning to Eibar each weekend to hunt, at least during the first months after you moved. Until what happened to Aitor. After that there would be no more hunting, no more trips to the hills. That was when the nightmares began.

You remember your father standing by the telephone in the house in Vitoria, gripping the receiver. He was squeezing it as if it were the neck of a chicken he was about to strangle.

'Aitor's gone missing in the hills,' he told you when he hung up, and the four of you gathered in the kitchen.

He explained that Aitor had headed up there at around midday and still hadn't come home by nightfall. Nobody knew why he'd gone; by that time he hardly ever went hunting. When you heard Aitor's name, for a moment your recalled his voice and that sneering way he had of calling you 'cuz', to belittle you. Up in the hills, especially in the hills, where no one could compete with him. You pictured him scaling the hillside, you could almost hear the jangle of the bunch of keys he always kept clipped by a chain to his back pocket. Only when the four of you all reached a certain altitude would he put his keys and the chain inside his pocket to stop them making a noise and startling the quail, or breaking the sacred silence of the pigeon fly-by. And you also remembered him asking 'Can you take this parcel to Vitoria?' one of the last weekends that you went back to Eibar to hunt with your father. You remember taking the parcel with trembling hands, not daring to ask what it contained. You hated him.

'First thing in the morning we're going up to look for him. We've arranged to meet in Plaza Unzaga at five,' your father said, looking at you.

'I'm going with you,' Libe said, but your father told her that the men would go alone, so in the end she had to stay home with your mother.

'Have you had a good look down there?' your father asked

you as you scoured your allotted search area in the Kalamua hills. Your father pointed to some small caves a few feet away down a steep drop.

You remember your father's fingers, his red knuckles and the look of desperation on his face. You wouldn't see that look again until many years later, when the strikes started at the factory in Vitoria.

'If Txo were here now, we'd find him in no time,' he said, recalling his old hunting dog, who he sold before the move to Vitoria. 'Have you had a good look down there?'

You said that you had, then immediately afterwards, your eyes met, and in that meeting of eyes, something hung in the air, dancing like scorched scraps of paper in a fire. To this day, whenever you look at your father, you can still see some strange specks like dust in the air between you.

You said yes, you'd already been down there, and together you moved on.

Unbeknown to you then, that lie would haunt you for many years. That was when the nightmares and the fear began. That was probably when the ball in your head began to grow too. Out of that lie.

The way down to the caves was too dangerous. And anyway, the fog was settling in and visibility was getting gradually worse. You didn't want to be the next in line to go missing in the hills. You were scared. Yes, you were scared and you didn't go down to those caves. You stuck your head over the edge of the steep drop to get a better look, but you didn't go down. You didn't dare.

'Did you have a good look down there?' your father asked.

'Yes. There's nothing there,' you replied, before

moving on.

The best lies are the briefest.

JASONE

11

I can feel your touch

Five words were enough to spur me on to start writing again. True, there was also a need to fill the gap left by my daughters, as well as a whole host of other feelings, anxiety and so on, provoked by the thought that the girl who had been gang-raped in Pamplona could have been one of my daughters; all these things had contributed to my need to use words to purge something inside me that simply had to come out. But the real reason, the fundamental reason, the one that finally lit the fuse were those five words spoken by Jauregi.

He turned up at the library, as he frequently did, to launch a book by a new writer, a rising star, according to him.

'There she is,' he said to the young writer as soon as I appeared in the foyer. 'It's worth coming to a book launch just to see this woman.'

I smiled, but it was rather a forced smile. 'Classic Jauregi', Ismael would have said if he'd heard that remark. I thought then that the only way Jauregi can conceal his shyness is by making a joke, that all his apparent chutzpah is just squid ink that he squirts out to cover up his nakedness. Joking is a way of gaining power over the person before him, of putting himself a rung higher on the ladder. And as so often before when Jauregi had made a similar comment, I had very contradictory feelings. I felt like slapping him in the face and, at the same time, sticking my tongue in his mouth. I've always felt very attracted to him, although I couldn't say why, whether it was something more than physical attraction or just the way he looks at me, a look that makes me feel I'm capable of doing more than just taking care of the girls and putting away their clothes. It's not so much his eyes that I've always liked as seeing myself reflected in them. His way of looking at me. Of seeing me. Yes, perhaps I actually fell in love with my own reflection.

Afterwards, he asked if we could meet for coffee, and I seemed to see again the gaze of the Jauregi I'd edited the magazine with all those years ago, the Jauregi I'd so often sat up late with in a bar talking about the book we'd just been reading or trying to decipher some indecipherable poem. The same Jauregi who could recite from memory the first paragraph of chapter 7 of Cortázar's novel *Hopscotch*: 'I touch your mouth, with one finger I touch the edge of your mouth, I draw its outline as if it were emerging from my hand...' and I would tremble when I heard him say those words. I often wondered how many girls he must have recited those lines to. Jauregi was a real hit with women, he would joke around with them all; it was his way of flattering them and, in a way, breaking down their defences. I remembered the ridiculous scene when, for the first time, I gave him one of my stories to read. I went over to him in the university cafeteria, plonked the story down on the table and ran off without saying a word because I was so afraid he might make a joke I wouldn't know how to respond to.

'There's something I've been meaning to say to you,' he said on the day he came to the library.

'If you want me to ask Ismael about his novel, forget it,' I said.

'How many times do I have to explain: you are infinitely more interesting to me than your husband,' he retorted.

At that moment, I wished what he had said was not just one of his jokes, but something he genuinely felt. With Jauregi, though, it's always been hard to know exactly what he does feel. He's pretty unreachable when it comes to anything personal. As if he kept his feelings in a strongbox. Even his lovers have always been a closely guarded secret. And they still are.

He then went on to offer me a job working with him, which was the last thing I was expecting.

'I'd really like you to help me edit the occasional book we publish, just now and then, I don't want to overburden you. What you do with Ismael's books is just incredible... I can feel your touch, you know?'

Five magic words: I can feel your touch.

From that moment on, I felt as if some long-dead person were stirring into life inside me. I said nothing. And what went through my mind during that silence were all the years that had passed since Jauregi had last looked at me or talked to me like that.

'Someone told me you write stories,' he said the first time we spoke. And a few days later, I had plonked that story down on the table, then fled like an embarrassed schoolgirl.

After that, we spent many hours together at the university and elsewhere, editing texts, talking about literature, reading out loud to each other the stories we ourselves were writing. Talking about the stories we'd like to write and about our favourite authors... He was more Cortázar, and I was more Cheever. He was more Borges, and I was more McCullers and Carver. And we both loved Ribeyro. I can feel your touch. He was the person best qualified to recognise my writing style. Perhaps that's what has always most attracted me to Jauregi, that he, better than anyone, can recognise my writing style, that he can recognise something else in me beyond my female body.

I remembered him in our university days, before he wore glasses, when, as well as editing the magazine, he was just as likely to be organising a concert or a poetry reading as he was a political demonstration. He always had something to do. Those narrow eyes of his seemed to be permanently trained on some point in the future, some plan. He was wearing that same impenetrable expression when he — either jokingly or seriously — suggested we join forces and set up a publishing house together. With Jauregi you could never tell whether he was being serious or not. He had often heard me and Libe talking about wanting to set up a publishing house. I remember all the feelings his invitation provoked in me. I saw myself working with Jauregi and I saw myself living with him, becoming his partner, all in the same package. It became impossible for me to separate one desire from the other. In that respect, I've always envied Libe. She has always known how to keep love and the rest of her life separate. She managed to escape the trap that all women are prepared from childhood to fall into, the trap that teaches us to paint everything with the varnish of *lurv*, to fill every compartment of our life with *lurv* until we drown in those wretched romantic floodwaters. It's the sticky spoonful of honey that keeps us trapped, whereas men learn to put romance in one compartment and leave the other compartments in their life quite independent, free from the sticky varnish of love. That's *why* they're so much freer. As free as Libe has been too, I think.

With Jauregi's unexpected invitation to collaborate with him after all those years, I felt my carefully compartmentalised life was about to be upset again. And I felt, too, that the other me I used to be when I was with him was resurfacing. 'Hey, I'm here, had you forgotten about me?'

Yes, he *had* forgotten about me. How could he not, buried as I was beneath all the years I've been the mother who looks after her daughters, the daughter who looks after her parents, the wife who looks after her husband. All those years filled with domestic smells, the smell of bananas and rusks and wet wipes, the smell of a cupcake-baking mother.

I can feel your touch.

Those five words were what helped me to finally shake off the effect of those decades of anaesthesia. And I remembered the years when I used to write and make photocopies of my stories to show them to Jauregi and to Libe and receive their enthusiastic praise; and I remember giving a copy to Ismael, when Libe left for Berlin and he and I started going out together, the two of us in his Renault 4L, late one rainy night, parked up in Armentia, and Ismael saying 'Hm, not bad', then tossing the sheets of paper onto the back seat and kissing me, slipping his hand under my T-shirt, down my trousers, and filling the car with condensation. I remembered all that, but not the precise moment when I stopped writing.

Libe warned me right from the start, from when I first became pregnant, that I mustn't give up all those things. She wanted to keep reading my stories. She asked me to send them to her in Berlin. I tried to explain that it wasn't easy to carry on writing. First off, there were the girls; above all, there were the girls. And then there was Ismael, who was always busy writing. By then, he'd asked for a leave of absence from the newspaper so that he could write full-time after the unexpected success of his first novel. 'Sh, be quiet, Daddy's writing, let's go to the park so that he can write in peace.' So that he could write his Great Novel. And then, after a few more years, there were my parents; my mother was the first to fall ill and then, immediately afterwards, my father, as if they were in a contest laid on by the Basque Health Service. And they both needed the help of their only daughter, Asunción. Until I finally came around from the anaesthesia, my world was all doctor's appointments, false teeth, denture fixative, wheelchairs, shower stools, XL incontinence pads, the fusty smell of an airless room, the smell of old age. My parents' decline coincided with my daughters' adolescence, and my anxiety when they started going out alone at night and when I found a small block of hash in my youngest daughter's trouser pocket. Where was I supposed to find the strength, the necessary concentration to write? Where was that touch of mine that Jauregi reminded me had once existed? Buried. Transformed into the rigid hand of a shopwindow mannequin.

I fell into a depression that remained equally silent and secret. And through all this, Ismael was shut up in his study writing his Great Novel, not even noticing my highs and lows. There came a point when I asked myself: How can he be so blind? How is it possible to be a writer without looking around you, without seeing what's happening right beside you?

He didn't even register my gradual return to life when I did start writing again. Even in bed, I tried to rekindle something that had burned out years ago, but my caresses went unnoticed. I would reach out to touch his belly, and he would stroke my hand, then push it away. He was somewhere else. His head was in another place.

In recent years, I've been up and down, I've fallen and scrambled to my feet again. What happened to me during that time was an earthquake that must have shifted the floor tiles in the kitchen, as well as the parquet in the dining room and in our bedroom, and the corridor walls. It was as if an underground train had passed directly under our apartment, a really noisy, clattering train full of conflicting emotions, potholes and hairpin bends, and yet Ismael didn't notice a thing; holed up as he was in his bunker, he didn't feel so much as a tremor. During that time, I went from hibernation, from the dazed state brought on by the pills I was taking, to the pain that returns once the effect of the anaesthetic wears off. And that pain comes weighed down with leaden words, so heavy they sink to the bottom. The ones you see when the tide goes out.

And the tide had finally gone out.

I can feel your touch.

With those words the tide went out several yards. The tops of the rocks began to appear. Jauregi could not have imagined the feelings those words would prompt inside me.

For a moment, I felt I was once again with the young man who used to look at me differently, who saw beyond my body and my skin.

Anyway, when he suggested that we collaborate, I asked him to give me a little time to think. I was afraid to say Yes, even though that was what I wanted to say, even though his words had struck a match inside me. So, yes, I asked him to give me a little time. He looked at me, but said nothing, as if sensing that the biggest obstacle to my saying Yes wasn't time but Ismael. How would Ismael feel about me going back to working with Jauregi as I had in our university days? How would he feel about his wife editing the texts of other writers as well as his?

I said goodbye to Jauregi on the stairs, kissing him on both cheeks, and again I felt torn between the simultaneous desire to slap him and stick my tongue in his mouth. Before he left, I said that I would prefer him not to say anything to Ismael about his proposal, not for the moment, not until I'd given the matter more thought. When I said this, I saw Jauregi's eyes light up. We were again sharing a secret, just between the two of us. Again. Just as, for years, we've kept secret that suggestion of his that we start a publishing house together. When he looked at me like that, he was recognising the Jasone who used to write. He seemed to be asking me to go back to that, to go back to writing. That's what he was saying without actually saying it. That's what he was asking me to do.

I couldn't get Jauregi's words out of my head all afternoon: I can feel your touch. When I got home and after having supper with Ismael, I told him I had a few work things I needed to finish and I stayed up into the small hours writing. That was my way of coming round from the anaesthetic. By starting to write again. Writing as a way of disinterring things, images hidden by time and by blind normality.

And so, after many such nights, I ended up writing something that, up until now, I've resisted calling a novel. And I felt the need to phone Jauregi and tell him Yes, I was finally ready and willing to help him at the publishing house, but the days passed and still I didn't phone, because what I really wanted was not just to work with him, but to give him my novel and have him read it. I imagined the typescript in his hands, I imagined his long fingers caressing the sheets of paper, and I got goosebumps. I couldn't understand why I felt it was so important for Jauregi to read my novel. Perhaps I wasn't so very different from Ismael, and I, too, was looking for a stage, for applause. Or perhaps I needed to seduce Jauregi, wanted him to slip his hand down inside my bikini bottom while I, hands tied, said No, No, when what I wanted to say was Yes, Yes.

I felt that Jauregi was waiting for me to write something, that what lay behind his offer to work with him was a desire on his part for me to start writing again. And I knew then that the day would come when I would appear before him, novel in hand. Whenever I thought this, though, I felt like a traitor. I couldn't have felt more guilty if I'd taken a lover.

Meanwhile, the only person I dared share the novel with was Libe. I sent it to her in Berlin. I knew how pleased she would be that I'd gone back to writing.

LIBE

12

The age-old battle

You take your seat on the plane and place Jasone's novel on your lap. You hold it as though it were the baby you've never had. Your mother would say the same. People are always watching for some maternal gesture in women who haven't had children, some clue that will betray the fact that, deep down, they wish they had. The age-old battle.

Your mother has a real talent for noticing what you don't have rather than what you do have. For making you feel guilty. Despite this, living at a distance for the last few years has brought you closer. Your mother finds it much easier to talk to you about certain things over the phone rather than face to face. When you're together or when she's with someone else, she can't find the words, perhaps that's why she spends the day preparing meals and putting them in Tupperware containers. She puts her words in there too, adding pieces of her heart to the spicy prawns or the red onion and pepper sauce.

She doesn't yet know it, but soon you'll be with her again. No one knows that you've brought forward your journey, that you're arriving this very afternoon at Bilbao airport. You'll simply turn up and phone from there, saying: I've arrived. You can't really explain to anyone what you're doing, because you haven't managed to explain it to yourself, despite knowing that behind what you're doing is that very ancient law, the one you thought you'd long since rejected, jettisoned. The law that says it's the daughters who should look after their parents, a law that resonates everywhere, like an echo in a cave.

'It's a small story, not one of those big stories,' Jasone says in the letter she sent along with the novel. And you wonder what the really big stories are. You remember the refugee camps where you worked. It's years since you slept in a tent, now your job is the bureaucracy of solidarity: setting up working groups, suggesting new strategies, coordinating policies, running meetings, preparing speeches, managing campaigns…

In recent years, you've only heard about the big stories from those camps down a telephone line or on your computer screen. And you know you're not where the big stories happen, because they only happen at ground level and you can only write about them by getting your boots muddy.

It's been a long time since you got your boots muddy, not since you rose to your current position in the NGO, and spend all your days at the desk in your office. Before that, your hand often used to clasp the cold hands of people with no roof over their head. Now you're far removed from all of that. And this has been like a mini-death for you.

You look at Jasone's novel, which you found utterly astonishing, and you realise that your best friend is closer than ever to revealing her particular truth, in a way she never has before, closer to freeing herself from all her fears and looking the truth in the face, while you have headed off in the opposite direction, moving ever further away from your own truth. You've taken a step back from all the things you've spent years lecturing Jasone about. It's as if the student had overtaken the teacher and were laying bare all her contradictions. Now, when it seems Jasone has finally cast off her role as everyone's servant and carer, along with any feelings of guilt she had about focussing more on herself, when she has finally managed to find her real voice, you — her feminist guru, her human rights idol, her revolutionary friend — are taking a big backward step. Guilt is now forcing you to return sooner than expected to your home, to your parents' home.

Or perhaps not. Perhaps it isn't a backward step. Perhaps that's where your place is right now, with your mother and father, among all the many small stories that accumulate around them. Perhaps now your story should centre on that, perhaps right now that is the place for your big story.

But you're not at all clear about this, you're confused, your principles are engaged in a wrestling match with a woman with long blonde hair and too much mascara. Woman against woman, women fighting each other, as people expect, as women have been taught to expect. Even in dreams.

The air stewardess has just asked you to fasten your seatbelt. You thought you already had. This happens a lot lately. You have your imaginary seatbelt fastened all the time. Sometimes you don't even need to have one on, imagining is quite enough, imagining that it's going to keep you strapped in, so that you don't even attempt to get up. The imagination is a powerful thing. It's enough for you to think you already have your seatbelt on for you not to do anything. Imaginary seatbelts work very well.

You think of all the little deaths happening in your own life, deaths that you take for granted. Nowadays, death turns up in a much more subtle way, in disguise, like modern-day hearses, which bear no resemblance to the long, black limousines of yesteryear. Death used to approach you head on and you could see it arrive, complete with first name and surname. Now, though, it arrives in a grey van, which could be that of some delivery man bringing you stuff bought on the internet, and it enters your life without you even noticing, stealthily deactivating you from within, generating all those little deaths of which you're more aware than ever, especially after reading Jasone's hard, honest novel. Jasone's uncomfortable novel. Because the truth is always uncomfortable, like an old sagging armchair with broken springs that stick in your bum when you sit on it.

For a long time, you were the family's broken spring. First, with your political militancy. You're going to get us all into trouble, your mother would say. And then with your homosexuality. A deferred homosexuality, which took you a long time to accept, and that your family still don't completely accept.

Jasone says in her letter that you've always been braver than her, and you know this isn't true. From high up in the plane you see everything much more clearly, every line, every curve of every road. The roads that shaped your life. At home, you were always the contrarian, the awkward broken spring, but what exactly have you succeeded in changing? What have you done in the last few years but run away? Almost twenty years ago, you had to flee. You wanted to. Propelled in part by your own acknowledgement of your homosexuality, but also by the political atmosphere, which was becoming unbreathable. The conflict. It sullied everything, including, in large measure, your ability to come out as openly gay. The people needed heroes, not dykes.

Your dream of setting up a publishing house with Jasone seems so far away now. You both really thought you could change the world by publishing books. And you have since tried to change the world, you really thought you could; that's why you joined the NGO and, seen from up here, that's the most transgressive thing you've ever done. But the grey hearse slowly hove into view, stifling your energy. Over the years, you've worked for various international organisations, in positions of increasing responsibility. And now, when you sit in your office with the heating turned up high, you feel you're at the epicentre of the very system you've so often cursed. It isn't what you dreamed it would be. You are Maupassant's fake necklace. The picture postcard punk of La Polla Records.

Jasone, on the other hand, has undergone a slow, silent revolution, with no masks and no disguises. Today, she's a new woman. You only have to see the deep mark left on the paper by every word in her letter. It could have been written in braille.

You're afraid. In the next few days, you'll be sleeping in your childhood bedroom. Without Kristin's warm body beside you. She wanted to come with you, but you said No. She's been wanting to get to know your country for a while now, but you've never given her the opportunity. You're afraid she'll like it and want to stay. So this time you'll be alone with yourself again in a single bed. And you can't be entirely sure that you know the woman who'll once again be sleeping in that bed. You don't know if you're the same one or a more saccharine, cut-price version. You feel this is the most dangerous journey you've ever made. Far more dangerous than trips to Uganda, Ethiopia or Ecuador. A journey back to your past, to your home. To your contradictions.

When the plane set off down the runway, you closed your eyes. You always get nervous at take-off. Your body is moving forwards, but it feels as if your head were being left behind.

After hearing the sound announcing that you can unfasten your seatbelt, you looked out of the window and saw that you were already flying above the clouds. You look down at your lap again and see that you're gripping Jasone's novel hard. And at that moment, you feel you're holding on to something that doesn't belong solely to her. The book contains someone who's addressing you as well. Someone looking you straight in the eye and stripping you bare.

ISMAEL

13

It wasn't me

On his own, your father seems like another person. It's never occurred to you that he could be afraid of being home alone. It's never occurred to you that he could be afraid of anything. Nor have you ever considered how important his wife's presence is to him. Without her, all of a sudden, he seems like a frightened little boy trying to mask his fear by speaking in a manly voice, the very one you learned from him.

It's been two weeks since you started spending the afternoons at his place, trying to write in your old bedroom, on a laptop. But that room weighs too heavily on you. You remember yourself there at fifteen, sixteen, with the door closed to keep out the smell of your father's Ducados, the smoke that would waft in from the living room, or so as not to have to hear him asking you one Saturday afternoon, 'Shouldn't you be out somewhere, don't you have any friends in Vitoria?' No, you didn't, and your father liked to make you feel that was your fault, as if it were easy to arrive in a new city at fifteen and make friends. You would often help him on a Saturday to clean the car, a Seat 131 Supermirafiori, which he looked after as if it were a museum piece. When you and Libe were little, back in Eibar, he would cover the back seat with a blanket so that you didn't get it dirty; and he almost never took the car on hunting trips, you almost always went in your uncle's old Talbot Horizon. On the rare occasions that your father did take the Supermirafiori, he always lined the boot with a plastic sheet for his muddy boots, shotgun, and the partridges or pigeons he'd shot. It was into that very boot that you would pack all your worldly belongings to take to Vitoria, leaving behind in Eibar all the things that didn't fit, like your childhood friends, or the smell and sounds of the square and the streets where you'd played since you were a boy. You remember putting away your things in the wardrobes of your new bedroom, feeling that you, like those clothes, were entering a dark and lifeless place. You can't write in there, the room where you wrote your first ever stories. So today you've decided that from now on, you're going to bring your father over to your place in the afternoons. You'll sit him down in front of the TV while you write in your study, just as Libe told you to do.

You go to pick him up, but instead of walking straight into the living room to say hello, you watch him for a moment from the doorway. He looks nervous, lost. And seeing your father like that reminds you of the period during the strike action at the factory; a crack opened up in him then too. You remember the day you asked your sister Libe what was going on. Someone had called your father a scab. Those were months of tension and silence at home. You remember your mother's silence. You've actually only just noticed your mother's silence. Seeing her in hospital, with that blue nightdress and that bruised cheek, has affected you more than you thought. Seeing her like that it felt as if she had lost some special superpower. She's not jumping to her feet, tidying things away, cleaning, hanging out the washing, or mopping the floor in zigzags. She's just there. And she seems to have shrunk. You don't recognise her. She's nothing like the woman who used to read the newspaper out loud to you all.

Now she seems like a woman you saw once, only once, crying to herself. One afternoon, back in Eibar, when you got home from school you found your mother sitting on the side of the bed she shared with your father, sobbing. Next to her, open on the bed, was the biscuit tin where she kept spare buttons. It was the first time you'd ever seen her cry. And the last. Your mother wiped away her tears, stood up and asked what you wanted for supper. You remember you didn't dare ask her why she'd been crying. You don't know what's brought back that memory of your mother, a memory you thought you had forgotten, but it's not mere coincidence.

Having seen her like that in the hospital, your mother seemed suddenly to have become a stranger. Not just Libe and Jasone, but now your mother too. How are you going to write about a woman if you don't even know those closest to you. It's as if you'd been condemned to live in separate rooms. Rooms with closed doors. You need to open a door, but you don't know which way to turn to find it. You're groping in the dark.

Remembering your mother in the hospital, you try to decipher exactly what it is you're feeling. You should feel sorry for her. But when you look inside yourself you find other emotions. And you don't like what you see. You're angry, furious. You're angry at your mother for having fallen over, for possibly having something wrong with her brain, for being ill, for not still being your mother. Because her absence is making you see the house and your father in a new light. Because leaving you in charge of your father in the afternoons has robbed you of precious writing time and further distracted you. And despite your best efforts, you're still finding it impossible to get inside the skin of the woman from your nightmare. You're angry at your mother for all these reasons. And you're ashamed to feel this way.

You've seen her looking weak now, and that image has thrown you into a world that never existed before. You always thought your father would be the first to die, that your mother would be widowed and would live on her own for a few years. Not only because your father is older than your mother, but because your father couldn't live on his own. And now, on seeing your mother in hospital, you've thought about what would happen if she died first. It would be a catastrophe.

Not only for your father, but for you too. And not only because you would have to take care of your father, but because you can't imagine that new world in which no one will wish you luck when you go off abroad to some book fair, or when you publish a new novel. A world in which no one will keep a folder of newspaper clippings from interviews or articles about your latest book. In which no one will bring you Tupperware containers of food. Spread out before your eyes is a whole new panorama in which no one is going to watch over you, look out for you. Look after you.

And it dawns on you that, in the presence of your mother, you are still a little boy. The mask of the intellectual, of the professional writer, falls away. You're naked. When you're with your mother, all of your weaknesses and fears come out, the ones you were never taught how to accept or recognise or show. Your selfish side comes out too, the side that makes you feel angry with her. And what might be your true voice, the one you've been struggling so hard to find in recent years, the voice of that little boy hiding behind the voice of a grown man. A boy who's scared, just like your father. Perhaps you're not so different.

'Don't leave him on his own,' your mother reminds you at every opportunity.

And you're surprised now not that your father feels scared, which is something you've been slowly getting used to the more time your spend with him in the afternoons, but by your mother's unceasing concern for your father, her need to know that he's okay, that he's not alone.

Your mother reels off a long list of orders each morning from her hospital bed, things that need doing at home, the meals that must be prepared for your father and how, so that you can relay it all to Nancy… But you're incapable of retaining it all, so yesterday you decided to film her on your phone so as not to miss any details or make any mistakes when you pass on the instructions to Nancy.

Today you arrive at your father's house with the video on your phone. After watching your father for a few seconds from the living-room door, you take a deep breath and ask him how he is. He replies with another question: 'What are you doing here at this time of day? Shouldn't you be working?'

Once again you feel the need to justify your work to your father. To justify your existence really. Because as far as your father is concerned, your work isn't real work. For him, work means getting your hands dirty and then smoking a cigarette with your colleagues on your break, wiping the sweat from your brow with the sleeve of your overalls. Exactly what his son does he doesn't know, but it looks like secretarial work. When you proudly showed him your first published book, he said: 'But it's written in Basque…' In your father's mind you won't be a serious writer until you're published in Spanish. It's important to you to show him your next novel once it's translated.

You find Nancy in the kitchen and ask her to take a seat next to you, to watch the video of your mother you filmed in the hospital. As soon as the device starts to reproduce the image and voice of your mother, your father appears in the kitchen. On hearing his wife's voice he must have jumped up from the sofa. You could never have imagined your father being this attentive to your mother's words. He hasn't once got up from the sofa to help her in the kitchen.

When your father sees the image of his wife in the video, he freezes, as if he were surprised to see his wife in that state, dressed like an invalid and with a large bruise on her face. He presses his hand to his forehead, as if he were feeling feverish, and returns to the sofa. When you go to get him, to take him back to your place where he'll spend the afternoon, you sense his breathing is more laboured than usual.

'Are you all right, Dad?'

Your father gets up without a word, his gaze fixed on the mirror in the living room. He doesn't take his eyes off his reflection. You look in the mirror, too, as if you might find there some unfamiliar landscape, and while the two of you stand gazing at the mirror, your father says something you can't fully digest:

'It wasn't me.'

'What wasn't you?'

'I didn't hurt her.'

'Dad, please, she's not like this because of you. Of course she isn't, you didn't do anything. It was her, she fell. It was an accident.'

'It wasn't me,' your father repeats robotically.

His image and yours, together, held inside the mirror's gold frame.

And then you have a terrible vision. You picture your father beating up your mother, knocking her to the floor, like the man in your dream knocking the woman to the ground. You don't want to be thinking these things, but that's the image that comes to you, damn it! You must be losing your mind. You must stop it. It's all that crap your wife puts into your head… This mania for turning all men into culprits. There's absolutely no reason to think that your father has ever mistreated your mother. It's all in your head, the head that no longer works properly, that can't function, that's contaminated. And yet, that image is so very real…

Looking in the mirror you have another vision: as well as seeing yourself and your father, you seem to see other men behind you. They all have your father's face. They could be your grandfather, your great-grandfather, your great-great-grandfather. It's like looking at cave paintings. And in the background you can hear '*I-ña-xio gu-re pa-troi han-di-xa*', as if the tune were coming from the AM band of the radio. And, over the music, those men repeat in unison: 'It wasn't me. It wasn't me.'

Suddenly, in that mirror you see both your guilt and your fear. The same fear you feel when a girl is found raped up in the hills, the same guilt you feel when you imagine your father abusing your mother. It's all there in the mirror. It's all connected. It all stems from the same place. From the same cave.

You tell your father not to feel guilty, but really it's you you're saying it to. You tell yourself you have nothing to feel guilty about. Maybe it's that bloody ball in your brain that's making you think these things, that's preventing you from writing. Maybe you're going mad.

You take your father home with you, but he's twitchier than ever. You find it even harder than usual to concentrate on writing, as if waves of your father's unease and nerves could pass from the living room through the gap of your study door.

'It wasn't me...'

He hasn't stopped all afternoon. Every time you hear a noise, you leave your study. You find him opening drawers, cupboards, sitting here and there...

'No, Dad, not there, that's a glass table.'

'Dad, no, that's the Thermomix, don't touch it, careful...'

'Not that door, Dad, that's the balcony.'

Your father is constantly moving about as if he wanted to scatter whatever it is he's carrying inside him into every corner of the house, like when he used to smoke and he would leave cigarette butts all over the place. Or like when he would arrive home having had a few drinks at the bar with his friends and he'd empty out his pockets wherever he happened to be. In the end, you manage to get him to sit down on the sofa in front of the TV, and you go back to your study. But it's impossible to concentrate, so not a word gets written.

After a few minutes you get up to go to the bathroom, and, as with previous days, you find the rim of the toilet bowl splashed with urine. You wipe it clean with a sheet of toilet paper, which you throw into the bowl before pressing the flush and watching the water carry it away down the drain.

There goes your novel. There goes your career.

14

The coins

You could always tell what state he was in after an evening in the bar from the way he opened the front door. If before putting the key in the lock he kicked the door with his foot, you and Libe would know that he was drunk and that it was better to stay in your bedrooms. He would leave his jacket in the hallway, delve his hands into his pockets and empty their contents into the glass ashtray on the table either there or in the living room, to avoid a shower of loose coins raining down onto the floor when he took off his trousers. You and Libe would wait for him to go into the kitchen before creeping out of your rooms and pinching a few coins. He never found out, or so you thought. 'Fry me a couple of eggs.' After a long night drinking, your father always asked for fried eggs. With crispy edges. You remember there'd be an orange yolk stain at the corner of his mouth when you'd go to wish him goodnight.

15

A perspex door

For two weeks you've been writing, to the best of your ability, about that woman. You're making progress, but very unsteady progress. Having your father at home is certainly distracting you, but there's something else. You're haunted by the thought of your father being an abusive husband, and feel guilty about it. You haven't forgotten what Jasone told you about your inability to feel her pain as if it were your own. And also on your mind is the text you found in Jasone's rucksack. In truth, you haven't been able to get it out of your head since you found it. That woman's voice. Maybe it can help you find the voice of the woman you're writing about. Perhaps she's the missing key, perhaps it's like first listening to a song in order to sing along to it later by yourself. You could try to carry that music into your text. So you leave your study, go into your shared bedroom and start rifling through drawers. She must have put it away somewhere for safe keeping. You have to find it. And when you spot a see-through plastic folder at the back of her underwear drawer, buried among knickers and socks, you feel like a hunter on a lucky day. A hunter with a good nose. A fine hunting dog. You grasp your prey, sit down on the bed and start to read again.

'The sound of a sliding door opening. Just describing it fills me with terror. I only have to imagine it for my heart to start pounding, for me to wet myself with fear.'

As you read on, your own heart begins to pound too. Those words describe in detail the scene that's been obsessing you recently. They describe a woman being raped. In the first person. And with every word, you can feel her breath in your ear. Terror pours from her throat. You can hear it as if you were there, as if you too could hear the sound of a transit van door sliding open, and the hairs on your arms stand on end as you imagine a tongue entering her ear, the sweet-sour smell of saliva in her mouth, imagining how every one of her orifices will be violently penetrated, until the damage extends far deeper than her body… Imagining her thighs prised open, her eyes clamped shut, how she doesn't resist, for fear of suffering more pain, and her silent pleading: 'Stop, stop, make it stop'. You can hear her humiliation as clearly as if it were an actual sound. You can smell it as if it were an actual smell.

And then you hear a dog bark.

And you push the typescript away from you.

You can't go on reading. You feel a familiar pain. Something has shifted beneath your feet. And you realise it's a pain you too have felt and that, for the first time, you're seeing reflected in this woman. Not like in the woman you've been trying to write about up until now, the woman who, when you reread what you've written, seems ethereal, bland, with no clearly defined edges, like water or air.

The same can't be said of this text. There's a pain inside

this woman that, in some way, you feel as if it were your own. And, at the same time, as you delve deeper into her pain, you feel guilty. It's a contradictory feeling that prevents you from positioning yourself in any concrete place, that buffets you from one side to the other, like a flag in the wind.

Reading Jasone's text, realising that it's left you feeling grazed, has also helped you to see that there's a Perspex door between you and the woman you're trying to write about. There really is a transparent, but very solid door between you. You still haven't felt her pain the way you've felt that of the woman in Jasone's text. And it reminds you of the door to Libe's bedroom, which closed one day, never to reopen. Could it be reopened? After all this time? The door to your sister's bedroom. There was a time when you and your sister shared a lot, but something came between you, and now you realise that, deep down, ever since that door closed, you don't really know who Libe is. And you get the feeling that you must find a way to get back into your sister's room if you're ever going to enter into the mind of the woman you're trying to write about. The same key fits both locks. It's the door behind which you might also discover the woman Jasone has become over the last few years, especially since the girls left home. Perhaps it's the Jasone who no longer tells you everything the way she used to. Jasone the author of these terrible words, which have shaken you to the core.

It terrifies you to think that such pain could have come out of her mind. She hasn't written anything in years, she gave up writing, you've never really known why. At first you had doubts about who the author of that text might be, but now, having read on, you recognise Jasone's voice, her way of writing, which you'd forgotten. It's a Jasone who is both recognisable and unfamiliar. Recognisable in form but surprising in content. You can't stop wondering why she's written about a rape and how she could have written about it as if it had really happened to her. Maybe that business with Eider and the girl found in the hills had affected her as much as it had you... Whatever the case, you're scared, and you're not sure what you're scared of. And that's unsettled you. Above all it unsettles you to think that the voice of the woman speaking in that story is the one you search for every time you sit down to write. It's her. At last you've found it. The only problem is that you didn't find it in your head, but in your wife's knicker drawer.

You're holding the typescript in your hands, but something is stopping you from reading on. There's something in those words written in the first person that disarms you, returns you to your worst nightmares, makes you feel again that familiar combination of crushing fear and guilt. Your heart is beating fast as if you'd just run all the way home from the top of Olarizu. And once again, out of nowhere, you hear a dog barking in the distance, a bark that reverberates through your whole body. But you quickly realise that it's not a dog barking, it's your father calling you from the living room.

You hastily put the plastic folder back where you found it. You look dazed as you head out into the corridor, still shaken by the terrible images you know will follow you.

Your father calls out for you again. His fear unsettles you terribly. Every time you hear his voice, firm but also frightened, you feel a creaking sensation, as if the ground beneath your feet were cracking open.

'Are you there?' he calls out.

'Yes, it's okay Dad, I'm here,' you reply in a trembling voice, swallowing hard.

16

He's just not a hunter

'He's just not a hunter,' you heard your father say angrily.

He was talking to your uncle as the four of you made your way down from the hills. It was one of those days when he'd told you off for startling the pigeons. A bad morning's hunting in which he'd wanted to try out his new shotgun but hadn't got the chance. One of those mornings when your father would throw his boots onto the kitchen floor when you arrived home at midday. One of those days when your mother would tidy up after him without a word and no one would speak or make too much noise for the rest of the day.

You were a few feet behind them and overheard what he said. And you felt a cartridge explode in your stomach. The wound still smarts.

'He'll have to be put down,' your father went on, and only at that point did you realise they were talking about Mendi. 'Yes, we'll have to put him down.'

Your father then turned around, whistled and shouted, 'Mendi! Come.' You didn't want to believe it could happen, but when your father was angry, anything was possible.

Mendi appeared beside your father and uncle, with that brown patch over his left eye. He was alert, with his ears pricked and his tongue hanging out, waiting for an order. As if surprised to be the chosen one for once. Ready and willing. Then your father took out his shotgun. A new shotgun he'd used for the first time that day. He hadn't had any luck with the pigeons, he hadn't been able to christen it properly. Mendi was still watching him attentively, wagging his tail, ready to obey your father's orders, to show him that he was a good hunting dog. And just then you ran over to your father and grabbed the shotgun with both hands.

'No.'

'Do you want to do it then?' he asked you. 'Here, let's see if your aim's any better than it is with the pigeons.'

'No, Dad, please,' you begged him.

'He's just not a hunter... He has to be put down. Aitor! What about you? Have you got it in you?'

Only one thing could be worse than your father killing Mendi, and that was for him to ask Aitor to do it and for your cousin to accept. Aitor took your father's shotgun, the almost brand-new shotgun. He took it in his hands like someone handling something precious. He had always liked guns. He ran his hand gently along it, inspected it back and front and, raising it to shoulder height, took aim.

'In the head?' he asked.

'Yes, in the head.' your father replied.

It was a single shot. Clear and distinct. An echoless shot. In place of an echo you heard a whimper, a moan that lasted only a couple of seconds.

And then all went silent.

An icy silence that accompanied you all the way home, and, in your case, returned every time you went near your father after that. It wasn't the leaves crunching underfoot; it was your trampled stomach, heart, and lungs. You recall looking at Aitor from behind, as you made your way back down the hillside. His confident, self-satisfied swagger as he went down the hill alongside your father, the jangle of his keys… You hated him with all your heart. He was chatting away to your father and uncle like he was one of the men. Your father and uncle listened to him like he was too. You followed behind them thinking about Mendi, the only one who'd ever walked beside you.

When Aitor went missing up in the hills, you no longer had a family dog. Your father sold Txo when he could no longer look after him.

'If Txo were here now, we'd find him in no time,' your father told you during your search for Aitor. Your father admired his old dog, the best dog he'd ever had. He was clever, brave, loyal. He never showed the love he felt for Txo to anyone else. He never spoke to anyone the way he spoke to Txo.

'Have you had a good look down there?' he asked, pointing to the caves.

Sometimes, when your father looks at you, you feel as if he's still asking you that question. Even today, every time you look at your father, or your father looks at you, you feel like he's questioning whether you've really looked.

You remember a map spread open on the wooden table at the hunting club. Your uncle marking with a red pen the areas where they'd already searched for his son.

'We need to widen the search area...'

'What was he doing up there on his own and so late?' one of the men asked.

Nobody replied. Nobody knew why he'd gone up to the hills. You imagined it must have been some sort of dare, or bet, or perhaps he went to hide something, a package like the one he gave to you. Aitor was fearless. How often had you heard your father praise your cousin's bravery. It had always seemed to you that Aitor did crazy things just to prove how brave he was, to fulfil other people's expectations. You've never understood why men are so impressed by idiotic risk-taking. You remember how, back when you were boys, your cousin jumped from the second floor of your school and broke his arm. When he returned to class with his arm in plaster he received a hero's welcome. Everyone wanted to sign the cast. And when you were a teenager, you remember him graffitiing *Gora ETA* all around town and leaving daubs of paint on his hands so that everyone knew it had been him. The kid with paint-stained hands was also considered a hero.

You remember your father looking at the map spread out on the table. His eyes frozen in a fixed stare. Often when you go home now to collect him you find him like that. Watching the television with a frozen stare. Your father, at some point, perhaps after the time of the factory strikes, opted for silence. And he remains silent, as if he were still crouched among the brambles with a shotgun in his hand. And you have always been afraid of breaking your father's silence. You have always sensed that his silence contains the essence of your relationship with him.

The news came via the phone, like the first time. By that

point, they'd been searching for two days. The call came late in the day, once you and your father were already home from your day's search on the hillside. They'd found him. A group who'd decided to revisit some of the territory that had already been searched. He was found at the entrance to a cave, unconscious and with a broken leg. He was taken to the hospital in a critical condition, but alive.

Your father was clutching the receiver the same way he had when they told him Aitor had gone missing.

'And where was he, did you say? Are you sure?'

They found him at the entrance to a cave. Someone had spotted a key chain a few feet away caught on a bush, close to a steep drop. He must have fallen down there, broken his leg and, realising that night was setting in, he must have dragged himself to the entrance of the cave, where finally he lost consciousness. When he was admitted, he was in a coma.

When your father hung up, he looked at you. And you recognised that look. He didn't say anything. Just that they'd found him. But that look was loaded with lead pellets. That look was telling you that they'd found Aitor in the area around the caves which you had supposedly checked two days earlier.

For a moment, you thought you heard the jangle of Aitor's keys somewhere in the background, like a macabre tolling of bells.

That look was the same one your father wore when he decided to put down Mendi.

'He's just not a hunter,' you remember him telling your uncle. 'We'll have to put him down.'

17

A stranger

'I saw your publisher today,' Jasone says out of nowhere, not looking at you, as she puts away the supermarket yogurts in the fridge — like someone throwing a stone and not bothering to see where it lands.

Ever since you found out that she's been hiding something from you, that story she hasn't once mentioned, you've been observing her more carefully. And you've started to notice some strange behaviour, like just now. Jasone talking to you without looking at you, when before she would always try to make eye contact, as if to check that you were really listening and not thinking about the work you'd left in your study.

'And what did your friend have to say for himself?' you ask.

'He asked about your health, he must have noticed you sounded a bit down the last time you spoke.'

'So now he's my doctor too?'

Every time she tells you she's seen Jauregi you feel a pang in your stomach. It's occurred to you before that the jealousy you feel when your wife talks to you about Jauregi is the one remaining sign of life in your relationship. Whenever you talk to Jauregi, he ends by sending his regards to Jasone. And you're sick of it. You just want an author-publisher relationship with him, a professional relationship. But your personal life always slips through the cracks of your conversations. You live in a very small country — too small.

'He told me to look after you. He sang *'Zaindu maite duzun hori'*, 'look after the one you love'... You know...'

'Yes, I know, classic Jauregi... Was he at the library? I didn't know he had a book launch.'

'No, I went to his office.'

You're lost for words. It seems very odd to you that Jasone would go to see him there... She's avoided the place ever since Jauregi started publishing you. As if for her it were a forbidden space. Jasone doesn't give you time to reply. And suddenly you look at your wife and realise she's taking more trouble over her appearance. As if she were emerging from a period of hibernation and recovering her youthful glow.

'He made me an offer a while ago... To help him with some texts. And I accepted.'

Your wife suddenly seems like a stranger. A different woman entirely. Not the Jasone who sits beside you in bed reading, or the one who speaks to your daughters on the phone, or the one who wanders into the bathroom as you're brushing your teeth, sits down on the loo and, with her knickers down round her ankles, tells you that you need to buy more yogurt. Out of nowhere another Jasone has reappeared in front of you, the one you first spoke to the day after Libe's arrest and who seemed totally out of your league.

She turned up at your parents' place, her hair drenched

from the rain.

'I'm Libe's friend, Jasone, if there's anything I can do...' she told your parents, in the living room, using the sleeve of her jacket to wipe away the rain dripping from the tip of her nose.

Her gestures betrayed a certain shyness, but she also seemed to you a very brave girl. She'd have to be brave to turn up like that at her friend's parents' place right after said friend had been arrested, even though she had never met them before, and had no idea what their politics were or what they would think of the Amnesty badge on her lapel. At that moment, she seemed completely out of your reach.

And, for a second, on hearing what she had just said about working for Jauregi, she once again seemed out of your reach. And she seems distant, very distant from you. Perhaps she's been working with Jauregi, editing other authors, for a while, and she's only just told you. Perhaps she has never stopped working with him since leaving university and you just never noticed. Perhaps it's more than just work they do together.

'Anything wrong with that?' she asks.

'But why you? Doesn't he have other people who could help him?'

'I guess he does, but he wants me. Anyway, I've told him that your writing is my priority.'

'You've talked about me? Are you serious?' you say, raising your voice. You feel a burning in your stomach.

'Don't be like that, it's hardly a secret. Jauregi knows you show me your books before giving them to him.'

You do not take this news well. Imagining Jauregi and Jasone talking about your work is worse than knowing that your wife might be editing other writers' work or that she and Jauregi might be about to rekindle their university relationship. It's even worse than discovering she's started to write again without telling you. While it's no secret that she reads and edits all of your books before sending them to Jauregi, you've never explicitly spoken about it before with Jauregi. And now you're imagining the two of them together picking holes in your texts, filling their mouths with the words they're both so fond of: subtext, ellipses, depth of character... Talking about you in your absence. Discussing your incompetence and ways to conceal that you're an intruder in their world, which is what you've always been.

Maybe this is what's given your wife a new lease of life. Talking in secret to Jauregi, imagining herself working with him. Maybe that's why she seems to have been reborn, why she's gone back to having a fringe like she did at university. Maybe that explains all those hours she spends out of the house. Is she having coffee with Jauregi? Maybe that's why she's given up on you in bed. Her body seemed to come alive again about a year ago, and she tried to rekindle the flame between you, but you could only offer a few tried and tested moves — you were no match for her. Your wife couldn't see that during that time you weren't really a man but a writer obsessed with a novel, a writer paralyzed by the fear of failure. And in the end Jasone gave up. These days she doesn't even bother trying. Maybe she looks for it elsewhere, with Jauregi. Maybe that explains the twinkle in her eye, which you hadn't seen in such a long time.

'And you didn't ask me?' you say, raising your voice. 'You should have asked me first.'

'Are you serious? Are you honestly saying that I have to ask your permission?'

You don't reply. And given the way she looks at you, holding your gaze for several seconds, waiting for a response, you sense that your silence has descended on her like a dusty old blanket. Once she realises that you aren't going to respond, she leaves the table and walks out of the kitchen and into the bathroom, slamming the door behind her. You don't know why she has to get so angry. You haven't said anything to make her angry. You don't understand women. How will you ever get inside their skin, even in fiction? There are simply too many things you don't know about women. They're all hiding something up their sleeve, something they'll never show, another side to themselves that's invisible to the eyes of men. You've lived with Jasone for going on thirty years, and, suddenly, you feel like you don't know her at all.

You're left alone at the table, making balls out of the breadcrumbs on the tablecloth, imagining the size of the ball growing inside your head.

JASONE

18

Fear is a difficult balancing act

Anger and rage can transform many things. They can make us move from words to deeds. They can give us that necessary final push. They can override our fear, or at least conceal it for a while. This is what happened to me after my initial fury at Ismael's response to the news that I'd decided to collaborate with Jauregi. An egotistical response, the seriousness of which I might not even have noticed a year ago. And the rage his response provoked in me seemed to remove a layer of feeling from me, a layer of fear that had always accompanied me.

A fear that grew stronger when my daughters left home, leaving me alone. When they left, I became completely obsessed with filling the yawning physical gap in the house. I had to reinvent their rooms, I couldn't leave them as they were when they were living there. The teddy bear on Maialen's bed, for example, had to disappear because it seemed to be constantly asking after her. Or perhaps I was the one doing the asking: 'How is she? Haven't you heard anything either?' Perhaps this was what propelled me into moving apartments. I needed to erase the backdrop against which we had been a family, where they had been my little girls, and which had since been transformed into something resembling a post-nuclear disaster: a sepulchral silence, with my husband spending all day in his bunker.

When we began the move, I often asked them over the phone if I could throw out this or that.

'No, Mum, don't even think about throwing away that leather jacket,' Eider would say, as if the clothes she used to wear at some point in her life contained a part of her, her essence, which might vanish if thrown away.

My whole story is ruled by fear. My youngest daughter's essence, though, which might be hiding in that leather jacket I wanted to throw out, knows no fear. She reminds me of her Aunt Libe. Libe had a similar jacket, the one she brought back from London and which did, in fact, contain her essence. Yes, Libe was like that too.

When my daughter told me she was going to Turkey with a girlfriend, I felt really glad to see how free and fearless she was, but, at the same time, I had to bite my tongue so as not to pass my fear on to her, the fear I've always felt, that we have always felt. I've never really known how best to respond, because I know that while a little fear could protect her, it could also paralyse her. Fear is a difficult balancing act.

I bit my tongue as I often had when they went out together at night, but I've never known if I was right to do so. I've always been full of uncertainties. Perhaps things would have been different if, instead of having two daughters, I'd had two sons.

'At least I had sons,' another mother at school once said to me, when the girls reached the age at which they could go out on their own. As if I were doomed to suffer twice over because I had daughters. I felt like telling her that more men than women die of drug overdoses or in car accidents, but I didn't want to shatter her illusion.

Nevertheless, I know what she meant. She meant the fear that both Ismael and I felt when we found out Eider was going to Turkey with a girlfriend, just the two of them. The need we felt to protect her. The same fear we felt on the morning after the San Fermín fiesta. Fear of men, fear that some man might harm them.

I remember Libe as a young woman, in the leather jacket she wore for years. The leather jacket she brought back from London and hardly ever took off. I remember a photo of the two of us standing outside a music venue in Bilbao, Libe in her leather jacket and me wearing a long baggy sweater. She's giving the camera the finger and sticking out her tongue. I'm looking at her. As I always have.

'You mean you fancy my brother?'

I remember her mocking tone, her laugh, when I mentioned that her brother wasn't bad-looking.

'Why are you laughing? Aren't I allowed to fancy him?'

'I don't know, he's not really part of our scene, is he? Did he really tell you he's a writer?'

When Ismael approached me and Jauregi on the pretext of showing us his stories, even though he didn't belong to our little world, I thought he wasn't bad-looking, as I'd said to Libe, and what really attracted me to him was the fact that he fancied me. Looking back, I realise that what I ultimately found most attractive, apart from him fancying me, was that he was completely removed from the intensely political atmosphere that was slowly closing in around me and in which all my university friends were involved.

Libe's arrest created a distinct before and after to my fear. After that, anything to do with 'the political struggle' filled me with terror. And that was precisely the moment when Jauregi asked me to join him in creating a new publishing house, but I thought even that seemed dangerous. 'I'd really like to work with you,' he said, but my fear outweighed my feelings of attraction for him. Nothing is more potent than fear. Not even love. Jauregi was heavily involved in the whole political scene that ended up with Libe fleeing to Germany. He was in charge of printing all the political pamphlets, he wrote press releases for the students' union... Creating a publishing house with Jauregi would mean plunging into that perilous world.

I found myself very alone without Libe and felt that, somehow or other, I had to escape from that scene. Without Libe, I felt afraid, felt like telling everyone that I had nothing to do with that world, or with the faces that stared down at me from the posters of political prisoners pasted on the walls of bars and streets. My fear told me that I belonged to a different team, that mine was a different struggle. I wanted to go back to being Asunción, the *niña*, the little girl, who went shopping with her mother at the local store in a working-class part of town; I wanted to reclaim those Spanish words, *yaya*, *yayo* and *niña*. My real flags were the overalls hung out to dry on the balcony, my father's and my uncle's. For a moment, I was glad to have been born in Toro, far from that war, and wished I'd lived there all my life. I could prove then that I hadn't done anything, that my hands had always been tied, like that girl in my fantasy lying on a lilo.

Fear was stronger than anything else. I rejected Jauregi's offer of working together. Even though I wanted to accept. Even though I wanted him.

Ismael represented neutral territory, he had nothing to do with that war, even though his sister had been arrested. He didn't have stickers on his folder bearing incendiary messages or protest slogans, he had photos of the basketball player, Essie Hollis, cut out from the newspaper. He steered well clear of political meetings, largely because his father had warned him, 'Don't get involved,' the same advice his father had followed when he decided not to strike even though half the workforce did. Don't get involved, he always said.

Ismael was always afraid of getting involved in politics. And his fear brought me security. The fact that Ismael didn't decorate his folder with stickers demanding freedom gave me my freedom. And so I distanced myself from that world, I distanced myself from Jauregi, I rejected his offer of setting up a publishing house with him, I rejected him and the possibility of working together, even though that was what I really wanted. And, one night, I let Ismael take me home in the clapped-out old Renault 4L he'd bought, and when we said goodbye he took my hand. I remember how our hands touched, exploring each other in the enclosed atmosphere of the car, as if they had a life of their own. I remember this with an intensity that still surprises me. The two of us silently watching our hands, our fingers gently entwining. Ismael didn't fill me with the insecurity I felt with Jauregi. I didn't have to prove anything to him. I simply had to *be*. I felt this was what it meant to be free. But for a long time, what I called freedom was possibly only a secure little playpen my fear had built around Ismael.

Protection and security come at a high price.

I saw all this much more clearly, however belatedly, after Ismael's tantrum, after the way he reacted to my decision to work with Jauregi, a decision taken without consulting him. His anger was very revealing. It became obvious that any decisions I'd made in recent years have always been made from within a tightly circumscribed territory. And always pending his approval. I had rejected the chance to set up a publishing house with Jauregi when that was something I really wanted to do; afterwards, I stopped writing and for years devoted myself to creating a safe territory in which Ismael could write, a territory that included my own contributions to his texts. And all those limitations I'd been imposing on myself, believing as I did in a purely fictitious freedom, finally exploded in that rape, in that description of my imaginary rape, in the scream my novel represented and through which I came to the realisation that for many years I had kept that rape locked up inside me.

Ismael's anger with me for agreeing to take on that editorial job with Jauregi so infuriated me that my fury transformed my fear into strength. Indeed, the very next day, I turned up at the publishing house holding my novel in my trembling hands, determined to give it to Jauregi. At that moment, I felt as if I were about to make a bonfire of all those fears, complexes and constraints. My anger seized hold of them and transformed them into action. I was shaking when I went in, but nevertheless determined and fully aware of what I was doing.

History always repeats itself, albeit in different scenarios and at different times. I arrived feeling as nervous as I had on that day in the university cafeteria when I decided to give Jauregi a story of mine to read. On that occasion, I plonked my story down on the table and, lost for words, ran away. It was not so very different on this second occasion. And I wonder what it was, on both occasions, that provoked such a sense of insecurity and nervousness. It wasn't just that I needed him to approve of what I had written, I felt it would be truly catastrophic if he didn't, if he thought it mediocre and beneath his expectations. Jauregi thus became the judge who would decide my worth, and I think now that this is what has always happened when I've been face to face with Jauregi because this is what has always happened to me with men in general, that I've always needed their approval in order to feel that what I was doing was worthwhile, that I've always needed to seduce them somehow (not sexually, but to seduce them nonetheless) in order to persuade myself that what I was doing had some value, some meaning. For me, their word, the word of men, has always been the final word, although that's a hard thing for me to admit now. Ismael's perennial 'hm, not bad' was doubtless part of the reason why I stopped writing for so many years.

For a moment, I saw myself at one remove, always telling myself that anything I did was only ever 'not bad' because I couldn't tell myself that what I was doing was actually very good; I saw myself spending my whole life afraid that I might be asked a question I couldn't answer; I saw myself feeling like an impostor, believing that I didn't know enough to be in whatever place or job I happened to occupy; I saw myself apologising for being good at something, saying thank you to everyone, playing down my role. I thought that the time had come for me to confront all of this and reveal the real me with my novel, and to tell Jauregi that, in my opinion, it was a good novel.

I had considered sending it to him by email, but I needed to see his face when I handed it to him. And so I arrived at the publishing house and strode into Jauregi's office, even though I was shaking like a schoolgirl.

'How lovely to see you,' he said, and doubtless added one of his usual compliments, which my nerves prevented me from registering.

'Here,' I said, putting the typescript down on his desk, 'I'd like to know what you think of it.'

'Goodness, this is a surprise, Jasone. You've no idea how happy you've made me.' And when he said this, he looked at me with eyes that were saying: you and I always knew, we knew the moment would come when you would finally confess that you were still writing, and I can't wait to read what you've written, it will be like reading your heart. 'I can't wait to get started.'

'Don't say anything to Ismael, will you?' I managed to say, then left the room at a run, just as I had when I'd met him that day at the university café.

I heard Jauregi call my name, but I raced off down the stairs without a backward glance.

I spent a few sleepless nights, waiting for his response. Sometimes I felt sure that, at any moment, I would get an enthusiastic phone call from him, but the more time passed, the more pessimistic I became, so much so that I began to regret even giving him the novel, having shared with him my secret and revealed myself to him stripped bare like that.

LIBE

19

You're here

Your brother is speechless, amazed, when you call to tell him you've just arrived at the airport. You can tell he is really pleased, more than anything because your being here will lighten his load. You arrange to meet up the next morning at your parents' apartment and you ask him for the number of your mother's room at the hospital, because the first thing you want to do is visit her.

When you go into her room, you are shocked at how much she had changed. You haven't seen her for almost a year, although, during that time, you've talked a lot on the phone, but she looks as if she's aged at least ten years. When you go in, she is bent over a bowl of soup, and as soon as she sees you, she puts the spoon down in the bowl, pushes the tray away, and sits staring at you in silence. She always used to tell you: Bring the spoon to your mouth, not your mouth to the spoon. At first, she says nothing, then after a few seconds:

'You're here.'

Those are the only words she can utter, barely giving them the rising intonation of a question. You smile and say:

'You know how it is, Mum...'

As if that will be enough for her to understand about the imaginary seatbelt, that ancient law, and the wrestling match, all of which had been going round and round in your head throughout the flight. Your sense of guilt because you haven't been looking after your parents.

'Carry on eating, go on.'

'No, I'm not hungry.'

After another few seconds of silence, you are suddenly filled with regret. You regret having just dropped everything in Germany and come running home. Why bother if now you have nothing to say? And then you feel guilty about feeling regret, you feel guilty about everything, as has always happened when you're with your mother.

'I assume someone will come and collect this,' you say, pointing to the tray.

No, no good. Your words sound as if they were taken from a catalogue of stock phrases. You should have embraced her, that's what daughters do when they haven't seen their mother for a year, especially if their mother has had a fall and broken her hip, but all you can manage is a kiss on the cheek, a polite kiss, and you don't even take her hand, as they do in films, or stroke her forehead, or rummage around in her belongings for a comb, because she needs someone to comb her hair. The only thing it occurs to you to ask about is the tray in front of her.

'I assume someone will come and collect this.'

She asks about your journey, but not about Kristin, she never does, you're always the one to mention her and, when you do, she does show some interest, she'd like to know more about this woman you share your life with, but prefers not to ask. You know this, which is why you tell her about Kristin with no need for her to ask, you want your mother to be able to imagine her, to know her, to feel reassured. Although whenever Kristin says she'd like to meet your mother, you shake your head: No, no, it's better if you don't.

And suddenly you feel that the closeness with which you talked on the phone when you were in Berlin has completely vanished, and that, now face to face, you have reverted to being the mother and daughter you've always been, the daughter who slammed doors, the mother who made a point of hoovering right outside your bedroom very early in the morning, when she knew full well that you'd not long since crept in after a night out. The mother who would open the blinds with a clatter, as if she were starting up a chainsaw. How distant she is from you again. Beneath her skin lies the silence of your home, it's there in her veins, as if introduced intravenously.

The silence of your home. A long silence, a silence so slender that it slipped through the cracks in the doors, through the half-open windows, up the pipes into the kitchen sink, filling the whole place with something like tear gas. An edgy silence, dangerously domestic. The silences of families are like cement: if they're not dealt with immediately, they harden into something that could once have been removed very easily but which now cannot be shifted. This is why you're planted so rigidly at your mother's bedside.

You will return to that apartment as soon as you leave the hospital. You imagine yourself arriving at the street door, calling on the entry phone, going up to the sixth floor, and you see yourself like the little girl you were, coming back from summer camp with a bag of dirty laundry. You remember the smell of home. Your mother used to put bars of perfumed Heno de Pravia soap in all the wardrobes, and in the cupboard in the hallway too. You remember the hallway. A gold-framed mirror, a little marble table, a crochet-work mat, and on the mat the porcelain figurines your mother has kept scrupulously dusted for years: the little boy with the fishing rod, the little girl sitting beside him looking up at the sky, and the swan, its neck still surprisingly firm and intact. Beside it sits the glass ashtray in which your father would often leave his loose change when he came back from the bar in the evening.

In the living room, in the glass cabinet, there's a bottle of JB whisky and another of Karpy liqueur. They've always been there and probably still are. Your mother used to take them out of the cabinet at Christmas and then immediately return them, the way the faithful bring out the statues of saints onto the streets in Holy Week. Safe in their hiding place, those bottles have been a witness to your life. Next to them, your mother keeps a biscuit tin. Except there are no biscuits. It's where she has always kept her buttons. You don't recall ever having eaten any of those biscuits. Your mother used to hem trousers, sew on buttons, mend zips... Seeing her there in that hospital bed, seeing her lost for words, you had the sudden thought that perhaps one day she had decided to sew her lips together too. You remember how, at one time, she used to put away a hundred pesetas a month in that tin, from your father's wages, so that one day she could finally afford to buy that faux fur coat to wear to Sunday mass.

'Have you been to see your Dad yet?' she asks.

'No.'

'Well, go and see him now. Don't leave him all alone.'

Don't do this, your Dad will get angry; don't do that, your Dad doesn't like it; don't shout, you'll disturb your Dad. Your mother was always afraid her husband would get angry, would lose his rag, would smoke ten cigarettes while watching TV after supper, worrying about the problems at the factory... She was always trying to stop the beast exploding with rage. Now she is urging you: Go on, go on, don't leave him all alone. And you realise that this is nothing new, but this is the first time you've seen your mother unmasked and the first time you've become aware of the tension, the fear. The fear she has always felt of displeasing your father in some way, of being blamed by him for something or other that had happened. He probably even blamed her for your decision to go abroad. Yes, you can imagine your father blaming her for your departure. 'You've always let her do whatever she wants, so what do you expect...'

Before you left for Berlin, your mother kept insisting, trying to persuade you not to leave.

'Don't go.'

'I have to, Mum.'

'Stay here, even if only for my sake,' she said.

And knowing your mother as you do, you know how very hard it must have been for her to articulate those words, words that emerged from her sewn-together lips. But you did leave. And now you've returned burdened down with guilt. Seeing her there in bed, disarmed and no longer disguised as a woman who can cope with anything, you feel that you have always failed her, that even when she asked you for help, not to leave her alone, you didn't listen. There was too much noise in your head for you to hear anything.

You remember the cork pinboard in your bedroom. Will the tickets for concerts (Toy Dolls, Jingo de Lunch, Bap!...) still be pinned up there, as they had been the last time you visited, along with various political stickers (*Rhythm and Fight, Free the prisoners*)...? So much noise. So much noise inside your head. How could you possibly have heard what your mother was saying? How could you possibly have realised that she needed your help? That you mustn't leave her alone in that prison on the sixth floor?

ISMAEL

20

Dad frightens me

Libe opens the door to you in her slippers, as if she'd lived there her whole life. As if she'd never left your parents' home. She kisses you twice on the cheek, 'Hello, bro,' and gives you a friendly slap on the back. For a number of seconds you carry on talking in the hallway without daring to look directly at each other, as if some danger lurked inside the other's eyes. Your father is still in his room. Nancy is helping him to get up. It's his day to have a shower, and ever since your mother was admitted into hospital he only lets you help him. He doesn't want another woman to see him naked, not even his daughter. You felt a wave of pride yesterday when Libe told you that he didn't want her to help, that instead he wanted you to come. You felt drawn to him in a way you'd never felt before. It's the first time you've ever felt chosen by your father.

And this morning you've come over to help him in the shower and to say hi to Libe.

'Do you want a coffee?'

You sit down at the kitchen table, where you used to sit to have breakfast when you were young. But now your omnipresent mother isn't there, warming up the milk, making toast. Now the one serving you a coffee is Libe, a strangely domestic Libe. In recent years, she's had the aura of an outsider, of someone who won't be staying long, the air of a visitor. Like those suitcases covered in old airport stickers. Today, watching her serve coffee from the Italian moka pot, she looks like a housewife, like your parents' hostess.

'How are you holding up?'

'Better now you're here.'

'I hope you feel a bit freer and have more time to write. How's that going?'

'Badly.'

'Really? I wish I could help you…'

You're surprised by your own openness. You don't usually open up like this to anyone. But sitting in this familiar setting with your sister, you suddenly feel like the little brother asking his big sister for help opening a tin or because he's having difficulties with his homework. Your big sister transformed suddenly into a second mother.

There's a feeling of release that comes from confessing to your sister that you're desperate. The secret that's been eating away at you emerges into the air from your belly, where it's doubtless been causing a tumour. It's a moment of relief.

'We'll have to see what to do when they give Mum the all clear.'

'What is it we're supposed to do?'

'I don't know, but if she comes home, I don't know how it'll work with Dad… I feel like she won't be able to get any rest. I'm afraid of leaving her alone with him.'

For a moment you read in your sister's look the same

suspicion that's been tormenting you and that at no point have you wanted to accept. The idea that your father hasn't treated your mother well and that he'll go on mistreating her, in his own way, until he dies. And this summary judgement of him, sticking this label on him, doesn't seem fair. Your father is a good man. He's a good man, isn't he? He's spent his life working for you all. He's loved you all — in his own way. He hasn't always been able to express it but he's always worried about you kids, and your mother... He's merely treated her the way fathers have always treated mothers. No better or worse than other men.

'Dad frightens me. More now, with his mind the way it is,' Libe admits.

'That's not fair, Libe. Don't say that. He's not an abusive husband.'

'I didn't say he was... But not treating someone well is a form of abuse, Isma.'

'Are you being serious? Dad wouldn't lay a finger on her.'

'I agree...'

'So?'

Your sister's unforgiving attitude shocks you. Neither of you has any right to judge your parents' relationship. How can you weigh up something that happened in the past with the eyes of the present? What right do you have? Sometimes you can't stand all that guff Jasone comes out with: the war, domestic abuse, the patriarchy... As if all the world's problems had been engineered by its male population. Your father went through some really hard times, especially around the time of the strike action at the factory. He smoked more than ever, sitting in front of the TV. He probably lost his temper a few times and didn't treat your mother with respect... But... He's your father. He's the man in the photo in the living room taken on the day he married your mother, when they were young and in love.

'Things add up over the years,' Libe replies. 'Seemingly small things, but when you add it all up they're big things. Like what happened with the coat. Do you remember? You probably didn't even notice, you were still young. I think it was one of the only moments Mum couldn't hide her pain from us. She'd spent almost two years putting some money away in the tin where she kept the spare buttons, to buy herself a coat. She'd asked Dad if she could put away a hundred pesetas from his monthly pay... She'd chosen the coat, she'd spoken to the shop... One day, when she'd nearly pulled together enough money, Dad opened the tin, took the money and bought himself a new shotgun.'

As you listen to Libe you're filled by the image of your mother sitting on the edge of the bed crying. The way she jumped up when she saw you walk in.

'Mum didn't complain about it,' your sister went on. 'One day I asked her about the money and the coat and she told me that he'd earned the money and he was within his rights. The words came out of her mouth, but her eyes weren't telling the same story. You know, I couldn't bear to look her in the eye. I think that was the day I began to think I had to move out. I couldn't stand being party to all that.'

Your sister is still talking about your mother and her own sense of guilt is steadily growing clearer. She says your mother found herself very alone so far from her home town, her friends. Isolated and vulnerable. At least in Eibar she had her sister, her girlfriends... But in Vitoria... Libe reminds you that she tried to join a sewing group, to make some friends, but your father wouldn't let her.

'He told her she already knew how to sew, and very well too, and that there was no need for her to join any group.'

Then Libe tells you — in that weary schoolteacher tone she puts on to talk about women's rights — that isolating women is a form of undermining them, forbidding them to go out with their female friends or telling them that they'll always end up falling out with each other. She tells you these are all ways of rendering women lonely and defenceless.

You can't shake off the image of your mother sitting on the bed, crying, the button tin open at her side. And then, suddenly, a terrible image elbows its way into your imagination. You seem to see your father raising the butt of his new shotgun to shoulder height and aiming at your mother. Bang, bang. You see your mother collapse to the floor, bleeding profusely, those godawful pellets expanding inside her body like evil spermatozoa. And you see yourself watching the scene without doing a thing. Yet again, exactly like in the nightmare that so torments you.

You see the bloodstain spreading across the bedroom floor.

You see your mother mopping the floor, zigzagging back and forth, cleaning up the leftover blood, as if to hide any trace of her own murder.

You shake your head to erase the terrible image from your mind.

And then your father walks in with Nancy. You stand up and take him to the shower unable to get those terrible images out of your head. As you help him undress — he leans on you as he slips one leg then the other out of his underpants — you wonder how it's possible to see in him both the ogre and the frightened little boy that he's become. When you see him trembling before he gets into the shower, afraid of slipping; when you see him like this, so weak, so flaccid, so defeated... You think that, deep down, he isn't the iron man he always seemed to be, but a human being who feels fear like anyone else. A little boy in men's clothing.

The image of your father naked in the bathroom pains you. It pains you that your father should witness you seeing him in this state. You feel as if you're standing before an enormous edifice that's collapsing before your eyes. It wounds you because of what your father has been to you. The walls of his house are coming down. Those arms, those wasted muscles. It's hard to believe they're the same arms that used to lift you onto his shoulders on your trips to Deba, to the beach. That mocking laugh of his. That guffaw — half laugh, half cough. Those legs can't be the same ones that used to scale the hills like a mountain goat. Your father, afraid to step out of the shower in case he slips; your father, afraid to be left alone in the house. Your father, asking for help, like a child.

'Don't leave him on his own, he gets frightened.'

'Frightened of what?'

Up in the hills, he would whistle the way shepherds do to round up the dogs.

He could climb the hills like a mountain goat.

And when you remember him up in the hills, that vulnerable image of your father suddenly disappears, and in its place appears a man who steals the hundred-peseta notes from your mother's button tin; who throws his hunting boots onto the kitchen floor, covering it in dirt; who sits down in front of the television with a Ducados cigarette in his hand, telling your mother that she never learned how to cook properly, not like his mother, now she really knew how to cook… 'I wouldn't feed these fried eggs to a dog…' And you shut your eyes tightly to stop seeing those upsetting images.

You sponge his back, very gently, not daring to rub too hard, as if your father's moles were landmines that might explode at any moment. There's something orthopaedic about your movements every time you help him to wash. You don't dare wash beneath the folds of skin or between his legs. You spend the whole time moving the sponge from side to side, zigzagging back and forth, exactly the way your mother used to mop the kitchen floor. But it's not tiles you're cleaning, it's skin. Sensitive skin that has lived for far too long beneath a suit of armour.

'Here, Dad,' you pass him the sponge so that he can wash between his legs, as he has on previous occasions.

He knows perfectly well that you have your limits, that beyond them the cave is too dark, too unfamiliar, familiar yet strange. For a moment, you seem to hear your mother's omnipresent voice:

'Run the hot water over his back, it eases the pain.'

And all the while you talk. You've never talked to your father as much as you do during these sessions together in the shower. Silence, in this particular situation, terrifies you. You ask him about the temperature of the water and the seat in the shower, if it's in the right position… You don't want your father to hear you struggling to swallow. You don't want him to hear your throat contracting at the sight of his withered skin, his limp, shrivelled penis.

You're an explorer, discovering a new world.

After his shower, your father asks you to cut his toenails. And it's only then that you realise that you've never cut anyone else's toenails before, not even your daughters'. Jasone always took care of that. And as you struggle to cut your father's toenails you become aware that cutting someone else's toenails is really quite difficult. You can't do it while facing the person. You have to be beside them. You're worried about nicking his skin. You get the same feeling you have about this woman you're trying to write about, the feeling of not knowing how to gauge if you're cutting too much or too little. That feeling that you're sitting at an awkward angle as you write about her, of not being in the position that would allow you to see what she sees.

You don't get the sense that you're cutting the nails safely until you place one of your father's legs on your lap, like a third leg. And it occurs to you that that is the key. You can't write about your main character if you don't put yourself in her position, if you don't see what she sees. You won't do a good a job until you're sitting clipping her toenails as if they were your own.

Seeing what she sees.

Instead of looking at her, as you've been doing up to now, you have to look at what she sees. That's it. And what does she see? She sees her attacker. Perhaps it's time to look at the man. To look at his face. Even if you have the feeling you already recognise him. Even if you know that the man, damn it, is going to have your father's face.

21

Arconada, I'm supporting him

You remember a scene in which your father is in the living room, watching the Spanish national side play a match. Libe walks in wearing a black t-shirt emblazoned with the word 'Resist'. Libe was always asking your father things that no one else dared ask him.

'You don't really want Spain to win, do you?'

Your father didn't feel the need to explain himself to anyone at home, apart from Libe.

Your father and Libe's relationship. One long competition.

'Some of our Basque boys are out there on the pitch too... Like Arconada, I'm supporting him.' he replies.

You pass by your sister as she leaves the living room and hear her mutter: 'Fuck Spain.'

22

It's not just his lip that's crooked

Ever since you saw your father's face in your nightmare, the memory of your cousin Aitor has returned with even more intensity. There's something that makes you connect him with the worst aspects of your father. You remember your cousin after the accident, with his crooked lip. The most visible physical scar when he left the hospital, having spent a month without recognising a soul. The lip that remained slightly wonky on the left-hand side, and which sometimes makes it difficult for him to speak.

'And his head? Is his head all right?' you overheard your mother ask your father as she served him his supper.

'He's not going to be able to start his course... Seems it's not just his lip that's crooked.'

When you found out that Aitor had left the hospital, you were relieved that you were already living in Vitoria. You wouldn't have been able to stand being in Eibar, fearing you might bump into him at any moment, around any corner; you still weren't sure whether he'd seen you on that first day of the search, and whether he might still have been conscious then. You hadn't actually met since he gave you that package to take to Vitoria. You were afraid he might accuse you of being a coward. The other reason you were glad you moved away from Eibar was because of the increasingly oppressive political atmosphere. Because you were afraid that at any moment someone would ask you to do something you didn't want to do. There was a saying that hung like a cloud over all young people at the time: 'We all have to give a little, so that the few don't have to give their all.' It was hard to refuse without feeling like a traitor.

Over a year went by without you seeing your cousin, but the moment would have to come. And it did. A year later, you were invited back during the local fiesta and, although you hesitated at first, you finally went. You spent the whole night fearing that, at any moment, Aitor would show up in some bar and say: 'So, cuz, are we allowed to know where you've been hiding?' And just as you were beginning to relax, after a few drinks, you spotted him, at the very end of the evening. You heard some shouting from inside the bar. You went in and saw Aitor with his crooked lip, drunk and shouting.

'*Gora ETA Militarra*!'

He was on his own. People were staring at him. Some turned their backs on him. Others were encouraging him, shouting back: '*Gora*!' But that young man was lost, he was all washed up, as your mother would say. It pained you to see your cousin like that. You watched him for a while and then left before he spotted you.

You again saw your guilt in that crooked lip, in that wild shouting. If you'd been brave enough to go down that steep drop, Aitor would have been rescued twenty-four hours earlier and the consequences wouldn't have been so grave. On seeing your cousin like that —like a madman, transformed into another person entirely — you wished he were dead. You wished he'd died up there in the hills. And at that moment, you reminded yourself that this wasn't a new feeling. Even when you and your father were out looking for Aitor you hadn't wanted him to be found. You'd wished he would disappear forever. And for the first time you acknowledge that it wasn't just fear that stopped you scrambling down to that cave.

23

Come on, if you've got the balls

The cursor is blinking defiantly at you on the computer screen. It's like a man challenging you to a fight, each blink is a hand beckoning you over and saying: 'Come on, if you think you're hard enough. Come on, if you've got the balls.'

You're holding Jasone's typescript. There's a pain in it that you recognise. There's a feeling of contempt and humiliation that reveals itself like the grainy patterns that show through if you write on a piece of paper resting on rough ground. Whatever the surface you write on, it always shows through. The ground we walk on and that's formed out of all the things that have happened over the course of our lives. Even the parquet flooring in the apartment we grew up in.

The pain that's distilled in that text brings you closer to a pain you recognise in you and your family, and which is leading you to discover some place in your very origins. It's not a new pain. It's a pain that impregnated the silence of your childhood home, the hot dinners and cold conversations of that sixth-floor apartment. A pain that has the same origin. That comes from the same cave. And you don't know exactly where that cave is, but you know that your father also lives inside it, and your cousin Aitor, and the effects his sudden, violent death had on you.

You feel like Jasone's story holds the key. A connection to a very domestic sort of pain. Reading it has made you look in another direction. Or perhaps you're looking at the same place but from a different viewpoint. As if you'd gone to sleep one day in your own house, but in the bedroom of another member of your family. You step out into the same corridor, but from another room. Suddenly, everything changes.

The condensed suffering in the story is propelling you up to the sixth-floor apartment where you lived as a child. The words of the woman in Jasone's story have driven you straight here, as if on a motorway, to your mother's all-pervading pain, as well as to your own. As if the two things were somehow connected. You don't understand why. You begin to sense that the rape Jasone describes, the pain, is actually the solid parquet floor of your childhood home. It's not new, it's not unknown to you. After what your sister told you about the button tin, the new shotgun, the sewing group your mother never ended up going to, you can't help connecting the pain of that woman to your mother's pain. You imagine every word on the page in your mother's mouth, the same mouth that one day she was forced to sew up with the needle and thread she kept in that old tin. You again see her sitting on her bed.

And there, inevitably, you see yourself. The boy of the house. The boy whose father would have liked him to be more of a boy. The boy watching his mother, waiting for her to make his supper. The boy who doesn't ask her why she's crying. Who knows he doesn't have to ask her anything. The boy who before long will learn to say 'those are women's things'.

And all this is somehow connected to the sense of guilt and fear that you feel when you dream about that woman, the one you watch but don't help. You recall Vidarte. A writer cannot write about what he already knows, he needs to write about what he doesn't know, and writing is the writer's way of finding that out.

And, without a thought, you type four words on the screen. Without thinking about what you're writing. Four words that pain you, move you. A mystery. Words like torches, which you sense could light up a dark cave.

'Gunshots in the hills,' you write.

And you sit there still and silent. And you feel afraid. As if you were leaning out over a precipice.

You sit staring at the screen. The cursor is still defiantly blinking, like a man beckoning you over and saying: 'Come on, if you've got the balls.'

'Come on, if you've got the balls,' the line echoes in your head.

JASONE

24

You're going to have to help me...

Seeing Libe again. Seeing her in the flesh coming out of the door of the apartment building where her family had always lived. The same door where I often used to wait before we went out together for a drink, where I would stand wondering what jacket she would be wearing, the same door we went in through with those two boys, when it was fiesta time in Vitoria, taking advantage of her parents being away visiting family in Eibar. I saw Libe come out and, for a moment, it felt as if time hadn't passed, that my voice, suddenly calling out 'Libe' was the same as it was then, slightly higher than it is now, more excited.

The first thing I noticed was her hair, which was much longer. Libe always used to have very short hair, spiky and defiant like her. Now her hair was long and straight, although her slightly old-fashioned use of henna was doubtless her way of adding a touch of the rebel to hair that had been tamed and domesticated by her current working environment of meetings and offices and jackets — jackets worn with jeans, but jackets nonetheless.

Seeing her like that, I wondered if she was happy in her job, if she was contented with her life in Berlin. Many years ago, she and I had dreamed of setting up our own publishing house, long before Jauregi suggested doing the same with me. It wasn't going to be a conventional publisher's, we were going to publish the kind of books others wouldn't dare to, we were going to put on readings and talks, and I've often asked myself what would have happened if the political situation at the time had been different. If Libe hadn't felt forced to flee. If fear hadn't left us paralysed like wax figures. If this war hadn't had such a constraining effect on us, hadn't set such limits on our future.

We gave each other a hug, only briefly, because we couldn't wait to see each other and talk face to face.

'Isn't Kristin ever going to come with you?' I asked.

'No. That would be too dangerous. She might want to stay.'

'Seriously? Have you actually considered that as an option?'

'Kristin wants to come, but I'm not sure how it would work out.'

'It's never too late.'

'What would we do here though? I'd have to look for an NGO and she'd have to find a teaching post somewhere.'

'We could revive old projects…'

Libe's eyes lit up when I reminded her of our old project. Talking to Libe again in person, there was no need to ask each other much about our respective lives because we'd always done that over the phone. And even if we hadn't, I don't think it would have taken us long. All those years of talking face to face had been training enough to know what each of us was thinking with no need to put it into words. We sat down opposite each other outside the café, and I asked after her parents. And I thought she was going to talk to me about her mother and father, but instead she spoke about Ismael.

'You know, I've been worried about Ismael. Has he still not said anything to you about his novel?'

'No, nothing. He's being very secretive this time.'

'You're going to hate me for saying this, but I think he needs your help.'

'But he hasn't even shown me anything yet...'

'I don't think he's got anything to show. You know what Ismael's like, he's never going to ask for your help directly...'

I can't honestly say I was surprised to learn that Ismael was suffering from writer's block. You could smell it in the air, see it in the way he would emerge from his office like someone emerging from a gas chamber, in his frantic searching through the books he asked me to borrow from the library, books he never finished, jumping from one to the other, as if he were pecking about in them, desperate for inspiration... No, I wasn't surprised to know he was having problems, although I didn't think they were as grave as the problems Libe was describing. What did surprise me, what most surprised me, was that Libe would think I had a solution to her brother's problem, because, just then, I didn't see how I could help him if I didn't even know what he was working on. I could read what he'd written so far and try to untangle the knot that was causing the blockage, but what else could I do? I couldn't write his novel for him. He's never been remotely interested in my writing. I couldn't give him what he calls one of the 'big stories'.

'You're the only one who can help him. You're so talented, Jaso. By the way, you must try and get your own novel published.'

'But how can I help him?'

'He needs your touch. Try and persuade him to show you what he's written and help him a little. I think he just needs a bit of a push…'

When she told me that I should try and get my own novel published, I was on the point of confessing to her that I'd already given a copy to Jauregi, but I didn't dare. I didn't want to say anything to anyone until I'd had a response from him. If he rejected it, no one would ever know I'd given it to him. If he accepted it, I would have to find the best way of breaking the news to Ismael.

The very moment she mentioned my novel, my phone rang. When I saw Jauregi's name on the screen of my mobile, my shoulders tightened, the muscles in my face tensed. Raising one hand and with a lift of my eyebrows, I silently apologised to Libe and told her it was a call from work, and Libe took the opportunity to visit the loo.

'It's just incredible,' Jauregi said, before I could say anything.

'Did you like it?' I asked, feeling nervous and excited, my heart pounding in my throat.

'Like it? I loved it.'

Jauregi's words were beginning to build a glass castle inside me, it was glittering so brightly it hurt, a very sweet pain, a much-anticipated pain.

'I'm so glad,' I managed to say, trying to contain my euphoria.

Then Jauregi went on:

'No, seriously. I think it's the best thing Ismael has ever written… It's so different from anything else he's done… And he's kept so quiet about it. Is it too early to speak to him, do you think?'

There are times when we build fictitious stage sets for ourselves, places where we would like to live. We even start to believe we actually do live there. But a moment comes when we realise that we're the only person living in that ideal land, that it doesn't exist for anyone else. Listening to what Jauregi was saying to me on the phone demolished a world I had always wanted to build and which, in the last few years, I thought I had been building, and with a great deal of effort too. A world in which I was considered to be someone capable of writing, valued for my talent. A world in which Jauregi was saying, although not in so many words, that he really wanted to read something I had written, that it was high time I showed him some new piece of writing, that my moment had come. And yet, suddenly, I discovered that he had not for an instant thought the novel I'd handed him was mine. Not for an instant had he acknowledged *me* as a writer. Perhaps not even when we were at university, where his interest in me could have had a very different motivation from the one I imagined. How naïve of me. And there was me thinking I was different from other women. Perhaps there had never been, as I thought, an intellectual attraction, perhaps he just wanted to get inside my knickers. The pain in my stomach was so intense that I found it hard to speak.

'No, don't tell him I've shown you anything, not yet,' I said. And seeing Libe returning to our table, I said nothing more and turned off my phone.

'Are you all right?' she asked anxiously, when she saw the look of shock on my face.

Feeling Libe's intense gaze fixed on me, I found it hard to speak. Finally, I did:

'I think I know how I can help Ismael,' I said. 'Although you're going to have to help me...'

25

Back to the sliding door

An abrupt change of scene. Squealing brakes, another sliding door opening and returning me to a dark reality. I was obediently going back to my rightful place, like a dog curling up at the feet of its master. It was like being batted out of the centre of the story and relegated, with a slap in the face, to the margins. I've often talked to Libe about that moment in women's lives when they find themselves up against a brick wall, having lived with the illusion that they were equal to men. With some, this happens when they get their first job; with others, many of them, when they become mothers; with others, on the day they meet a boy they think they've fallen head over heels in love with and who ends up raping them in his car; 'Stop it, stop it!' they plead, but he carries on and eventually they just let go, feeling utterly humiliated, not even wanting to recognise that they are being raped. That moment. That slap. That abrupt run-in with reality and your place in that reality. With me, that moment arrived by phone and in the voice of someone I had once thought really valued my work.

It left me utterly deflated. My pride deflated, my dreams

deflated, plummeting into the void, like a clothes peg dropping to the ground. The pain caused by the realisation that Jauregi had never seen me as someone capable of writing, that he hadn't, as I thought, been waiting for the day when I would hand him something written by me, that all this existed only in my mind, that pain made me wish I could be rid of that novel the way someone who, after giving birth, wishes she could be rid of an unwanted child, a child born of a rape.

And I didn't need to think much. The best solution would be to hand the novel to Ismael, to offer it to him so that he could use it in his own new book, or publish it under his name. It was best just to let go, to let go, and pretend you're not being raped, like so many girls in so many cars.

I knew he was desperate and incapable of getting into a woman's mind, which is what he really needed to do. This would all be easier now that Jauregi thought the novel was Ismael's. In a way, this was a relief. I would finally be free of a problem, of the headache that had dogged me all year. I wouldn't have to confess anything to anyone, I wouldn't have to hide anything, no secrets, no existential doubts about what to do with what I'd written. More than that, I would be able to save Ismael from total failure, a failure he would have found unbearable. Unbearable for him and, therefore, for me.

Deep down, though, that feeling of relief only served to disguise a void, a sacrifice, a small death to which I was, as Libe told me, once again opening the door. I felt again as if I were walking along a street at night alone, walking quickly, afraid to break into a run, afraid someone would uncover the white skin beneath my clothes, vulnerable, unexplored territory. Once more I heard the sliding door of a white transit van opening and felt myself falling into a black hole, into the void, my hands and legs tied. And someone was carrying off my most intimate self. Stealing it. Imagining Ismael making use of my novel opened up a great void in my stomach, as if a flock of birds were pecking away at my innards only to fly off with little tiny pieces of them in their beaks.

'Are you mad?'

Libe couldn't understand my decision. Libe wouldn't accept it, she couldn't.

'You have to help me,' I pleaded. 'You're the only one who knows I wrote it. Just don't tell anyone else.'

'Do you realise what you're doing? I can't allow it.'

This, she told me, meant another small death, and she couldn't be a party to it. What I was intending to do was a backward step, a sacrifice she couldn't allow me to make. She said angrily that I had to publish that novel and that something more than my career was at stake. This wasn't just about me.

'If you submit, we will all take a backward step,' she warned me gravely, as if she were suddenly speaking on behalf of all the women in the world. As if she were addressing a square full of women through a megaphone. 'It's your book, your voice. They can't steal it from you.'

I heard Libe's words, and I both agreed and disagreed. I knew she was right, but being right isn't enough. My pride had already been trampled into the dirt, and Ismael's need was clearly urgent. I had to do it. With Libe's help or without it. And so I went ahead. That night, while Ismael was brushing his teeth, I took the novel from the drawer where I had hidden it until then.

When he came over to the bed, I held the typescript out

to him.

'These are just a few notes for the story about a woman I've been writing on and off for a while now… They might help you in your research… There might be the odd detail you could use in your novel,' I said, before he got into bed.

A few notes, the odd detail… I was trying to make it seem like it was no big deal. I tried to speak in a neutral, detached voice, although as he reached out to take the typescript from me, I felt as if he were tearing my skin off in strips. And when I handed it to him, I was surprised by the nonchalant way he took it from me. I was struck by how unsurprised he seemed, by his lack of any desire to know more.

'Thanks, I'm sure it will be really helpful. Can you email it to me as well?' he said and put the typescript down on the bedside table, as if I'd just handed him a report or a list of library books. He didn't even ask me when I'd written it or if I'd gone back to doing my own writing. He didn't ask me anything, he treated it as a matter of no importance, and I felt like the most stupid person in the world. After more than a year of writing in secret, afraid of quite what I don't know, Ismael didn't appear to care whether I was writing or not. He simply accepted my offer of help, as he always did. And he made me feel that this was basically my function in life: to offer him help, to encourage him, to support him… 'You "new Basques" are very good at that kind of thing.' With those words, he had put me firmly in my place. In the margins. In my proper place, as Libe had warned me. Another slap in the face.

From then on, every time Ismael came out of his office, I had to bite my tongue to keep from asking him if he'd read it. He made not a single comment about the text, about my novel.

He didn't even say if he'd liked it. I felt like screaming, but instead went into the kitchen and beat some eggs; I felt like pinning him to the wall in order to extract some information from him, some response, instead, I stood in the bathroom silently removing my makeup, while all that emerged from his mouth was the white foam from his toothpaste. His silence pained me.

And that pain made me aware that I was not perhaps being totally honest. The pain inflicted by his silence was telling me that my objective in handing him my novel might not just have been a way of helping him. After being faced with Jauregi's indifference, what I was really trying to do was to get Ismael to recognise me in the words I'd written and to respect me for having written them. To say something more than 'hm, not bad'. For him, finally, to see me. That's what I really wanted, although I didn't realise this at the time. Yes, for him finally to see me. For him to push aside — like pushing aside brambles on a mountain path — the body of the desirable woman I had once been to him as well as the body of the mother I later became, for him to see beyond lover and mother and see me. Yes, finally see me, fuck it, *me*.

ISMAEL

26

Like scraps of scorched paper floating to the ground

You see him there, sitting in front of the television like a waxwork figure, and you wonder how your father ended up like this. You want to know just when he started to lose his memory. Certainly, what happened to Aitor hit him hard, as did those terrible months of strike action at the factory. It was then that he started to opt for silence as his weapon to protect him against the world.

Aitor's death. The untimely death of his favourite nephew, the great hunter. He never could get over what had happened up in the hills and, after Aitor's death, his gaze always made you feel guilty. As if he knew this was what you'd wanted all along.

Aitor's nightly performances, shouting '*Gora ETA*' in streets and bars, continued. After his accident, Aitor began going around telling the whole town that he was an ETA militant, and even that he had weapons and explosives hidden up in the hills. Nobody believed him. They all thought the kid had simply lost it. What a shame, such a fearless, capable young man, now one of the town's oddballs. 'Look, that's the guy who says he's a member of ETA when he's drunk.' You imagined people going around saying things like that. And again, like countless times before, you wished that Aitor had died at the entrance to that cave, that the fall had knocked him cold. That he'd disappeared from your life forever, long before he did.

And he did finally disappear. You came to think it happened because you had so often wished he would. One sunny August day, at noon, a loud explosion was heard in the building where Aitor lived with his parents. The police said the young man had been handling explosives in his room. After his death, the Guardia Civil found a cache of weapons and explosives very close to the caves near where you'd searched for him a couple of years earlier.

You felt as if you yourself had placed that bomb in his hands.

Aitor's death coincided with the strike action at the factory. Your father, one of the very few who didn't strike, would arrive home looking very tense, very cross. He lost a lot of friends. You clearly remember the day they daubed a graffiti next to the entry phone calling your father a scab. From that point on, your father opted for silence.

Now he spends the day in silence in front of the television. He looks like a waxwork figure. You ask yourself how your father would tell his own story, where he'd begin. It would certainly be hard for him to give an overview of his life, because while your father does hold on to a whole collection of information and events, he wouldn't be capable of relating them to each other. The story as told by your father would be something like a telephone directory, one piece of information after another, one event after another, with no connection between them, no cause and effect. He wouldn't tell a story, because it's not possible to tell a story without connecting everything up, without stitching one thing to another. You need a well-stocked button tin, like the one your mother had, to tell a good story. But as far as your father is concerned, things just happen and that's that. He doesn't see events stitched together through emotions, through feelings. Things just happen. Get busy making things. Make, work, produce. Those are his mottos. That's his vision of life: be born, work, die.

He spends the day in silence, as if he were waiting for the pigeons to fly past. And that silence, ultimately, is like his way of punishing you. Your father barely looks at you, and when he does his eyes still contain that same question: 'Have you had a good look down there? Are you sure you looked properly?' And he makes you feel guilty. Guilty about everything. Not being the son he wanted, not working like a man, not being a good hunter, being a coward, singing songs by Itoiz with your sister, not having 'the balls' your sister has always had... Even now, every time you unintentionally catch his eye, when you can't avoid his gaze, you can still see particles floating in the air, like scraps of scorched paper floating to the ground. It's your manhood in shreds.

You watch him sitting there, his hands resting in his lap. You remember those hands with their square nails showing you how to load a cartridge into a shotgun, those hands gently stroking the new shotgun bought with money taken from a button tin, those fingers stained yellow from all the Ducados he smoked, those nails that came home from work black...

You don't remember receiving a single caress from those hands; the closest thing to it was a pat on the back. And if he wanted to show a little more affection, he would thump you harder. That was the only way he knew. Those are not forgiving hands. Even if they wanted to be. They aren't hands that caress. Even if they wanted to.

And for a moment, thinking about those hands, you feel a pang deep inside you. The pain you've felt since childhood at your father's contempt for you, because you didn't turn out as he hoped, the pain at having lied to him and everyone in order to conceal your cowardice. A pain that's led you to defend yourself as well as you could. A pain you have to purge, to spit out. The way that woman spits out her pain in Jasone's story. However different, that woman's pain and your own are connected at some point. You just don't know quite where.

You watch him sitting there, in that armchair, and all you manage to do is sigh and go back into the kitchen to make your afternoon coffee. As the coffee brews in the old filter coffee machine, you take a moment to look out of the kitchen window. They're back again today. The birds. A murmuration of starlings moving apart and coming together again. As always, you're mesmerised, unable to take your eyes off them. Perhaps the birds themselves are mesmerised too. Perhaps that's why they all follow the same route. It's as if they were entirely focused on the movement they have to make so as not to break up the group.

The fear of breaking up the group, of being expelled from it.

That's what killed Aitor.

You put a couple of biscuits on a plate beside your coffee,

and you carry the tray back to the living room and your father. You can see him from the door. You can see the sleeve of his dressing gown and his hand on one side of the armchair and his white head visible above the chairback. You stay there for a moment, not daring to go over to him. But in the end you do go and stand before your father. He's sleeping with his head on one side, his mouth half open, and a white stain at the corner of his mouth. Staring at your father's closed eyes, you cannot contain yourself. The words catapult up out of your stomach:

'Would you really have preferred me to be like him? Would it be better to die while handling some explosive?'

Your throat hurts. The pain rises up from your stomach and tries to escape from your mouth. You feel uncontrollable rage, you feel you've always been a victim of your father. You hate him with every ounce of your being. In that moment, you wish your father wasn't just sleeping. You wish he were dead. You want to tell him that he's no good for anything anymore and that you'll have to have him put down. Take a shotgun and shoot him dead.

'In the head?'

'Yes, in the head,' you hear from somewhere in the distance.

Then, suddenly, a loud bang makes you jump, both you and your father, who's woken up with a start. The cup of coffee you were carrying on the tray now lies in pieces on the floor. And the coffee is spreading across the parquet. Without a word, you fetch a cloth from the kitchen to mop it up, beneath the watchful gaze of your father. With your father's eyes on the back of your neck.

27

The pearl necklace

They would meet up on Saturday afternoons. The two couples. Your parents and a colleague of your father with his wife. Fernando and his wife. You never knew her name. They'd always say 'We're going out with Fernando and his wife'. Almost always they went for a stroll in town, and usually ended up having a bite to eat. Your mother would put on her pearl necklace. You remember the smell of hairspray in the bathrooms on Saturday afternoons. You and your sister would wait for them to leave before putting out the crisps and soft drinks that you'd bought with your own money on the table in the living room, then collapse onto the sofa and watch TV. The house was yours on Saturday afternoons. Only on Saturday afternoons.

'Aren't you going out today?' Libe asked one Saturday when she realised your parents weren't getting ready. After the strikes at the factory, your mother never wore her pearls again. And your father and his Ducados took over the living room.

28

The great mystery

You hadn't been expecting Jauregi's call. He never usually calls you without texting first to see if you can talk. Today you get his call while you're staring at your computer screen. You have two documents open. The one Jasone sent you, at your request, and the one you started writing two days ago. You've only written four words: 'Gunshots in the hills.' You haven't opened the document in which you were trying to get inside the skin of the woman from your nightmares; you're missing something, some key, to really get inside her head. You still haven't hit upon the right way to reach inside her mind. What you've written so far now reads like a collage made out of counterfeit banknotes.

When the phone rings, you're just thinking that you have two remaining options: give up and confess all, or blindly forge ahead and present Jasone's text as if it were your own. You have her permission, but the mere thought of going through with it makes you feel awful. Could you really go on looking Jasone in the eye day after day? Could you really do interviews without feeling utterly ashamed?

'I'm sorry to call you out of the blue, but the printers are telling me we won't meet the publication date if we don't send them the book as soon as possible... A little birdie tells me you're sitting on a finished novel.'

You don't know what to say. That little birdie can only be Jasone, but why would she tell him that? Why is she convinced you're going to use her text? Maybe Jasone has found it easier than you have to accept you using her work and putting your name to it. Does she really think you're that lost?

'And apparently this time you've unlocked one of the world's great mysteries: what goes on in women's heads, no less!'

Jauregi laughs, it's just one of his jokes, but you feel as if you had been punched in the guts. All your muscles tense. You can't tell him the truth. Out of nowhere you remember your father's gaze fixed on the back of your neck while you were mopping up every trace of coffee from the floor. There he is, waiting for you to do something worthwhile, like when he used to wait to see if you were loading the cartridges into the shotgun correctly. And you're Mendi, wagging his tail, desperate to show your father that you do know how to hunt. There's no way out. You can't wait for someone to put a bullet in your brain. You can't be made to look a fool in front of your father, in front of Jauregi, the world. Jasone's text is your last chance. You swallow hard before replying, at the same time running the cursor back and forth over Jasone's novel, imagining how those words would sound in your mouth.

And at last, you take a leap, blindly forging ahead, like when you told your father there was no one in the area that you had supposedly searched.

'Yes, I have it here,' you say, quickly falling silent again. The best lies are also the briefest.

Perhaps this novel isn't what Jauregi was expecting. It really stirred you up because it's about something that's been obsessing you lately, but perhaps it's 'too feminine' and he's going to tell you it isn't what readers expect of you. But it's your last card, your last chance.

'I'll send it today,' you say brightly and put down the phone almost before he has time to reply.

You're a piece of shit, you think as you hang up. And with this thought sticking to you, to your fingers, you send Jasone's typescript off to Jauregi and, without a second thought, move the cursor over to the other open document.

'Gunshots in the hills,' it begins.

With your self-disgust lodged firmly inside you, and without the pressure of knowing that someone is waiting to read what you've written, now, now you really do begin to write, with an open heart, with words that leave your fingers hand in hand with each other.

And suddenly on the blank screen there appears, word after word, a story you've held in for far too long. As you write you can feel the south wind caress your face, so gently it hurts… As you write you can hear the dead leaves crunching underfoot as you make your way across the hills on that first day of the search.

Your fingers don't stop typing, as if they had something very important to tell you. In the story, a boy and his father are looking for a young man lost in the hills. The boy approaches an area of caves, and something glinting in a bush catches his eye. He thinks it might be a used cartridge that's got stuck there, but, on closer inspection, it's a chain attached to a bunch of keys.

The boy stares at the chain and its bright gleam seems to pierce right through him. And just then he hears his father's voice asking him if he's had a good look around the area, and he, without taking his eyes of the keys, says yes, he has. That there's nothing there.

As you write, it feels like your words are keys opening a door. Aitor's key chain. Aitor's keys. First, you saw something glinting, then you realised it was his keys. You froze. And it was then that your father asked:

'Have you had a good look down there?'

Perhaps if he hadn't asked, if you hadn't felt obliged to reply quickly, if you had thought twice about it, you wouldn't have dared to lie. But your father's voice drove right into your chest, a voice with square fingernails, and, without thinking first, and with a coldness that still surprises you, you quickly looked away from the bunch of keys and replied:

'I've looked. There's nothing here.'

And the pair of you moved on, leaving the keys behind, leaving Aitor behind, leaving behind part of your innocence and welcoming in an era of fears, nightmares and guilt that have pursued you to this day. You told him there was nothing there and you carried on walking across those dry leaves, hearing them crunch underfoot, feeling as if you were walking over dead bones. A crunching sound that won't leave you.

You stare at your computer screen. And the words pour out of your mouth on their own:

'It wasn't me,' you tell your reflection on the screen. 'It wasn't me.'

29

The crossword

Your father with the newspaper spread out on the kitchen table, open at the crossword page, while your mother prepares supper. Your father reading aloud the clues he can't solve.

'"Correct and genuine." It starts with a p and has one, two, three, four, five, six letters.'

'Proper?' your mother replies, looking at the crossword over your father's shoulder and drying her hands on a tea towel.

Your father checks to see if the word fits and, on seeing that it does, writes it down in the spaces, pleased with himself, convinced that he came up with it.

30

It's no longer your voice

You've barely set foot inside his office and Jauregi is congratulating you. He's beaming, his narrow eyes almost closed. His opinion has always mattered to you, so at first you feel pleased, momentarily forgetting that you didn't write the novel you sent him a few days ago. You sit down opposite one another, the table between you covered in piles of paper.

'The truth is you've surprised me,' he says. 'I don't think you've ever shown the depths of a character in quite the way you have here.'

You're surprised too. You didn't expect praise like this from Jauregi for something Jasone wrote. And as he talks about the novel, as he picks out what for him are its greatest merits, as you watch Jauregi's eyes light up in a way you've never see them do in response to your novels, you start to feel a burning sensation somewhere between your chest and your stomach. And the pain keeps intensifying. You've never seen him get this excited about any of your novels. The strained smile you're wearing is eventually wiped from your face when he asks you to also thank Jasone.

'You can really feel her hand in the edits this time. You're a lucky man. You two make a good team.'

It's like he's thrown a bomb at you and it explodes in your lap. You want to say Yes, he's right, but you can't stop your mouth curling into a sneer. Perhaps it isn't such a well-kept secret after all. Perhaps all these years Jauregi has thought that your books wouldn't be as good if it weren't for Jasone's edits. Perhaps he thinks all your books were written by her.

You want to say something that won't make you look ridiculous, exposed; you want to come across as cool and assured, but the burning sensation in your stomach is getting worse. And you can't stop your mind diving back into your university days. You recall Jauregi sitting in the cafeteria next to Jasone, and looking at you as if you were an intruder. Telling you that he'll publish your story, but only because Jasone asked him to. Maybe he's thinking exactly the same thing now. That he'll publish the novel precisely because she's written it. That the novel in which Jasone's hand is most noticeable is your best work.

After that, you stop hearing Jauregi's voice. All you can hear is the voice of the woman speaking to you from Jasone's novel. Suddenly, it becomes very clear that her voice doesn't belong to you. It's moving off.

You leap to your feet, you have to get out of there.

Jauregi accompanies you to the door, still talking about dates, cover designs, book launches. But you aren't listening to him. You have the feeling that the door is growing narrower, just like the space in your throat where the air passes through. You're going to suffocate. And once again you can feel the ball in your brain growing ever larger, on the point of exploding and ending your life.

You say goodbye to Jauregi with a cursory nod and, on hearing the door close behind you, you stand for a moment out on the landing. An image comes to mind of Jasone in her youth, back when she would write her stories and show them to you and wait nervously to hear what you made of them. She would watch you as you read, as if trying to tell from the look on your face if you were enjoying them. You suddenly remember her eyes awaiting your verdict, and how important it was for her to know that you liked what she was writing. You remember her reading, always reading, underlining sentences, jotting them down in the notebooks she carried in her pocket. You remember Jasone looking at the world and writing it down. There was nothing she enjoyed more.

And then you remember her later, after you were married, helping you with your writing. And in between there is a gulf, a black hole devoid of memories. When did she stop writing? Did she ever stop writing? You've never asked her about it. You've never given it any importance. And you realise that, until Jauregi gave it his blessing, you didn't properly appreciate her novel. Her 'notes'. Why are you seeing them so differently now?

And then another image smacks you hard across the face. You see yourself opening a biscuit tin. Inside it, among buttons of all shapes and sizes, is a wad of one hundred peseta notes held together with an elastic band. And you take them, you steal them and leave the tin open on the double bed. You imagine Jasone sitting on the bed crying, staring at the empty tin.

You have to sit down on the stairs.

You feel as if you were slowly edging closer to the source of your nightmares.

After some thought, you stand up, turn around and knock on Jauregi's door.

LIBE

31

Take a step back and start again

Ismael opens the door and shows you into the kitchen, almost without saying a word. As if he wasn't in the least surprised to have you turn up at his apartment without warning. As if the two of you had arranged this in advance. As if he'd guessed that you would come there in order to persuade him not to pass off Jasone's novel as his own. As if having failed to convince Jasone, you had decided to try and convince him.

'Aren't you going to offer me a cup of coffee?' you ask, addressing his back while he walked ahead of you down the corridor.

'I only have filter coffee, and I don't know if you like that. I really should buy a new machine…' he says, pointing to the coffee machine full of freshly-made coffee, as if the machine had been expecting you too.

'How's the novel going? You know, if there's anything I can do to help…'

Ismael says nothing, still staring at the coffee machine.

'Thanks, Libe, but, for the moment, there isn't going to be a novel. I'm just not ready yet to get inside that woman's skin.

There's something I need to do first.'

You look at your brother, your little brother, he seems withdrawn and nervous, as if he felt uncomfortable in his own kitchen. What he's just said has both surprised and cheered you in equal measure. And you realise that your brother is speaking to you in a voice you had quite forgotten. It's the voice of the person who used to be your little brother. Your little brother Ismael has returned. You used to hold his hand when your mother sent you off together to buy bread. He would grip your hand very tightly. And you would do the same. He enjoyed being with you, he felt safe. Suddenly, you can see again the little boy who used to play with the plastic bag of milk, moving the liquid from side to side, feeling with his little hands how the bag changed shape, growing fatter on one side and thinner on the other.

You recall how, many years later, in a newspaper interview, he talked about the need for a writer to combine the voice of the child he once was — the essence that appears in the first drafts, which is where you find true creativity and playfulness — with the voice of the adult, the one that appears later on and picks up all the toys in the room, correcting and imposing order and discipline on those drafts. You can only write by combining those two voices, he said in one of those interviews your mother cut out and saved in a folder.

Yes, that voice has reappeared. Where has your brother been hiding that voice all this time? He must have suppressed it because he was afraid others might hear in it all the fears he's kept hidden away throughout his life; the desire to burst into tears, the desire to go cartwheeling down a hill, the desire to dance, to kiss, to play… To reveal all his fears. Where has he been keeping that forgotten sensitive little boy all these years, the one who loved to sing with you, who secretly enjoyed playing with your toy kitchen, always afraid your father might see him?

'It's not easy to talk about anyone if you don't have a clear idea of your own viewpoint,' you say.

'Anyone would think that you and Jasone read the same books,' he says, smiling, and you smile back.

The two of you hardly need to talk. His smile reminds you of Sundays when you were children and you used to go to mass, and how, when you walked back to your pew after taking communion, you'd be greeted by your brother pulling a silly face. He made a point of going up to take communion first just so that he could greet you on your way back with that daft look that always gave you the giggles. You used to find it really hard not to burst out laughing. Where is the Ismael who used to pull those silly faces? Where is he buried?

'But, yes, you're right. I do need to step back a little.'

When your brother talks about taking a step back, you know what he means. He's talking about something you feel too, about going back to the beginning and setting off again along a path already travelled, but this time knowing something you didn't know before. Setting off from a new position that allows you to look around. Getting to understand yourself first so that you can then understand how you relate to everyone else.

When you escaped to Berlin, you were only thinking of yourself. You weren't thinking that you were leaving your mother alone in hostile territory or abandoning your best friend in the middle of a war zone. You were intent on saving yourself, giving little thought to the fact that every movement we make generates other movements in the people around us. That we are interdependent and bound together with twine. Raise one arm and the person next to you will raise their leg. You've always felt that Ismael has only ever thought about himself, about his career, his dreams, completely forgetting that Jasone has her own career and her own dreams, but then you yourself haven't really been much better. Without realising it, you've been dragging a lot of twine around with you. You've strangled more than one desire with the decisions you've made. Along with some of Kristin's desires. She's been wanting to leave Berlin for a long time, but for an equally long time you haven't allowed her to.

Your relationship isn't so very different from the kind of power relationship you've often talked and read about. Every relationship is based on power. So is love. Especially love. Someone always has to be the first to say the words 'I love you'. They are the losers. Whatever the other person's response, they are basically saying: 'Yes, I know.'

Today, you wonder if perhaps, with Kristin, you're reproducing your parents' relationship. If perhaps you're the one who makes the decisions and Kristin the one who accepts them. Kristin has been wanting to leave Berlin for more than ten years now, eager to visit Spain with you, to find out if she likes it and then, possibly, start anew, but you've always refused. As if you were your father. And you've hated yourself for this. No, perhaps you're not so very different from your parents.

'Do you think Mum would like to come and live with me for a while? When she gets out of hospital, I mean,' you ask your brother, although this was really a question you were asking yourself.

'What, in Berlin?'

'No, not Berlin. Kristin and I could come and live here for a while.'

'There's no way Mum would leave Dad on his own. Even if the house was on fire, she'd go back in, so as not to leave him on his own.'

'Perhaps that's precisely why it would do her good to spend some time with us. And Dad wouldn't be alone. You could carry on taking him to your place in the afternoons... It would be good for you two to spend a few hours together on your own.'

'No, I don't think so... I think it would be best if I went to see him and we spent the afternoons together there. I rather like the idea of writing in my old bedroom, *from* my bedroom, which has long been my place in the household.'

'The bedroom of the boy in the family.'

You look at your brother. Your brother looks at you. For the first time in ages, you look each other in the eye. Your little brother. Suddenly you feel as if you had recovered the brother you used to sing along with to those Itoiz songs, the brother you would ask to help write down the titles of the songs you were listening to at the time. You'd go into his room carrying a handful of cassettes. 'Come on, brother, help me write down the names of the groups.' And together you would write, in biro, the titles of the songs you'd recorded onto a 60-minute cassette. Thirty minutes each side. Side A and side B. Police, the Ilegales... You remember saying to him: 'Keep your writing small, otherwise you won't get all the titles in,' checking every word he wrote.

You were inseparable until the day you closed your bedroom door. You slammed it shut then, because you and your brother no longer had anything in common, no longer belonged to the same team. It would probably all have been different if you'd been two boys or two girls. You could probably have shared more things then.

You place your hand on his shoulder and squeeze it a couple of times, as if you were trying to send him a message in Morse code. Then he makes some off-the-wall remark about the filter coffee machine. He says you can take it home with you if you like, that it makes the best coffee in the world, but that it's a bit antiquated now. That he needs to buy a new coffee-maker. Perhaps the sort that uses coffee capsules.

'Still the same old Mr Fancypants, I see," you say, smiling.

This was your way of giving him a hug.

He's your little brother, damn it, and you love him.

JASONE

32

It isn't that I fancied Jauregi, I wanted to *be* Jauregi

The number of times I've accused Ismael of being blind, of failing to see all kinds of things, the number of times I've told him that in order to see beyond the surface of things, you have to make an effort, that normality renders the very foundations of reality invisible. And that's true, but the truth is that I, too, have been blind for years. I've been equally blind to the fact that my life has been shaped by a long-established mould, that I have faithfully played the role of lover and carer to Ismael and my daughters. I only began to see this when I started writing again and emerged from an anaesthesia that had lasted years.

And yet I found it even harder to understand my relationship with Jauregi during all those years. What did I feel for Jauregi and why? I only saw this clearly on the day he rushed into the library, panting and distraught, his shirt hanging out of his trousers.

'What the hell is Ismael talking about? What's this nonsense about him having no plans to publish and that the novel isn't even his?' he asked, his voice unnaturally high and breathless.

I said nothing. I couldn't believe Ismael had told Jauregi the truth. For a moment, I felt proud of him. For a moment, I thought my husband had cast off the layer of fear that has always paralysed him, the fear of failure that, in the last few years, has turned him into a vulnerable creature full of self-doubt. I thought he had overcome his hunger for success at any price, his need always to be the winner. But, above all, I thought he'd finally recognised me and decided not to deprive me of the recognition I deserved.

I suddenly saw a vast plain spread out before me. A huge empty space in which I could start again with Ismael. Perhaps the moment had come to go back to that car in which our hands had touched for the first time. Twenty fingers so entwined that it was hard to tell which were mine and which were his. To start again from there. To build something together out of those bare fingers.

I said nothing. For the first time, I didn't feel under pressure to respond to Jauregi. For the first time, I realised that I could remain silent before him without feeling uncomfortable. Without having to prove anything.

'So that novel is yours, is it?' he asked, looking at me with uncharacteristically wide eyes.

I felt that a long-awaited moment had arrived. Jauregi was finally going to recognise my talent.

'Yes,' I said, trying to conceal how proud I felt.

Suddenly, I seemed to see Jauregi unfiltered, with none of his usual circumlocutions, none of the humour he used to sugarcoat any words he found hard to say. His eyes were no longer the narrow eyes that were always hiding away behind some joke, some funny comment. Indeed, they looked as if they were about to pop out of his head.

Jauregi looked at me for a few seconds. I waited for his words of praise for my novel, for his congratulations... I even waited for him to burst out and say that I must of course publish the novel under my own name. I was hoping that, for him, at last, the important thing was the book and not who had written it.

'Well, you'll have to try and persuade him. He can't just withdraw like that. Everything's ready to go. All the machinery's in place. Jasone, please, you have to help me.'

Not for one second did it occur to him to ask if I was thinking of publishing it myself, or even to suggest that.

'Doesn't it matter to you that he didn't write it?' I asked.

What I actually wanted to ask was: 'Doesn't it matter to you that it's my book?' But I didn't dare.

'You've always been there in all his books. And it's not that different this time, is it? He has to set aside his pride.'

Ismael's pride. But what about mine? What should I do with mine?

This was the first time I had ever seen Jauregi so lost, poor thing, not knowing what to do. With nothing to say. No wry comment to make. And I thought about him, about what I feel for that man, what I've felt throughout my life. What is it that has drawn me to him ever since we met at university? Seeing him so lost, so taken aback by Ismael's decision, so desperate to publish the novel regardless, I thought that perhaps it was no longer so important to me to have his approval, the approval I'd been looking for all my life. Because what was it I've always wanted from him: Love? Sex? Affection? No. No, all I've ever wanted was his approval. His acceptance. From that day in the university canteen when I plonked my story down on the table and then ran away, from that very moment, all I've wanted was his YES in capital letters, his COME ON IN, JASONE, his invitation to the world of the chosen ones. And suddenly, at a stroke, after learning of Ismael's decision, which would mean, I assumed, his liberation from Jauregi and from other people's opinions, I, too, felt liberated, and finally understood what it was I felt for Jauregi: it wasn't that I fancied Jauregi, I simply wanted to *be* Jauregi; to have the power to decide, to believe in my own worth not just because others believe in me, but because I believe in myself. Seeing the bewildered expression on Jauregi's face was a revelation. So he wasn't so very powerful after all. In order to have power, he, like me, needed other people to give it to him.

For a moment, I no longer felt the need for him to recognise me, to acknowledge me, not even for him to publish my novel. I could publish it myself. I could *be* Jauregi. I could set up the publishing house I'd always dreamed of and publish whatever I liked. I didn't have to ask anyone's permission.

Perhaps the time had come to make that bold proposal to Libe. Time to book Kristin's air ticket. To be strong. Together.

ISMAEL

33

Another sleight of hand

Sitting in the kitchen, waiting to hear the sound of the street door opening at any moment, you stare at the filter coffee machine in front of you. There it is still, even though for some time you've found that machine somehow discomfiting. And for the first time, as you look at it, you ask yourself why in all this time you haven't thrown it out. You can only think of one reason: it's always been there. That's why it moved with you from the old kitchen to this one, and why it remains part of your daily backdrop. Because it's always been there. And that had seemed an important reason.

You're listening out for the sound of the door. Jasone is due home from the library at any moment. In front of you, on the table, some loose pages typed in Times New Roman. Jasone's work. You've decided you're going to return it to her, in person, physically handing those pages back to her. You'll try to make her understand with a gesture, realising now that you'll struggle to find the words to explain what has happened, your decision.

You'll struggle to find the words even though you are a

writer. Or perhaps precisely because you are a writer. It's not the same thing talking to a person while looking them in the eye as talking to a computer screen. Generally, those capable of one are incapable of the other.

At last she arrives. The sound of the door closing makes your heart race. She walks down the corridor, accompanied by the jangle of her keys. You stand up from your chair and she appears in the kitchen before you, carrying the freshness of the street on her cheeks.

You look one another in the eye without saying anything. Two writers without words. One in front of the other. The silence that falls between two people when everything is felt, not spoken.

Jasone turns to look at the pages on the table, as if to ask what they're doing there. You pick them up and offer them to her. It's your way of telling her that they're hers, that they don't belong to you.

Jasone holds out a hand, not in order to take the typescript from you, but to take the hand holding it. You put her novel back down on the table and hold out your hand to her. Before you know it, your fingers are entwined.

And that's when you remember it. The first time you two ever touched. Her hands were the first part of her body you caressed all those years ago, her soft hands. You drove her home, and when it came to saying goodbye, she held out her hand and you took it, and you spent a few minutes stroking each other's hands, there inside the car, fingers entwined, the back of one hand cupped in the palm of the other, all your bodies' sensitivity concentrated in the tips of your fingers, in that pressing and releasing of palms. Jasone's powerful hands.

Back then you noticed their softness. Only now do you realise the power they were concealing.

You feel guilty about it, and for a moment you visualise your own fingers with square nails, horrible nails like your father's. But you realise that the more they caress Jasone's hands, the softer and rounder they become. It's as if you were back inside that car, as if your entwined fingers were suddenly indistinguishable, as if you had initiated another sleight of hand, one that makes it possible for your nails to feel square and round at the same time, one that makes it possible to feel like both a victim and a culprit at the same time, without that supposing any contradiction.

Jasone unlaces her hands from yours and goes to the bedroom, all without a word. You don't speak either. You are both writers, yet neither of you can find the words. Or perhaps it's precisely because you are writers. You can only find the right words, leaden words buried inside of you, when you sit down to write.

34

And the rest of the flock will follow behind you

Jasone's novel is once again in your hands. She left it on the kitchen table, although, before going to the bedroom, she put her rucksack beside it, as if marking out her territory. You run your fingers across the pages and for a moment it feels like you're still stroking her hands, and as you stroke them, you also note that the ball in your head is softening, becoming malleable, taking on a new shape. And out of nowhere they appear. Perhaps you had one eye on the window because you knew they were going to appear. The starlings. They fly in from the east, forming a grey cloud that constantly changes shape. Swift, sometimes sudden movements, which all the birds follow in unison. You still can't understand how they manage to keep the group intact. Who tells them which moves to make? It's as if from birth they'd received an order that would remain lodged in their mind forever, one they would rigorously follow, as if it were programmed into them.

You watch them closely, trying to work out which one of them dictates the changes of direction. And you realise that there's always one that decides to change course, and that the rest follow behind. You feel your heart start to beat faster then, you can hear the thud of your own heartbeat. You must go back to your study at once, to write using those fingers with their newly rounded nails. Finally, to write.

'Gunshots in the hills.'

You need to get that old story out, the story you've grown up with, to extract it the way one might extract a shotgun cartridge from the brambles. By crouching down and getting your hands scratched. Only by telling yourself that story — one about dogs barking, pigeons, shotguns, muddy boots and biscuit tins — will you discover where you learned to see the world from; only by recognising the source of the voice you reserve for your father will you one day be able to get inside the skin of the woman from your nightmare. Only then will you be able to change course. And with any luck, once you do, the rest of the flock will follow behind you.

DEDALUS CELEBRATING WOMEN'S LITERATURE 2018 TO 2028

Dedalus began celebrating the centenary in 2018 of women getting the vote in the UK by a programme of women's fiction. In 1918, Parliament passed an act granting the vote to women over the age of thirty who were householders, the wives of householders, occupiers of property with an annual rent of £5, and graduates of British universities. About 8.4 million women gained the vote. It was a big step forward but It was not until the Equal Franchise Act of 1928 that women over twenty-one were able to vote and women finally achieved the same voting rights as men. This act increased the number of women eligible to vote to fifteen million. Dedalus' aim is to publish six titles each year, most of which will be translations from other European languages, for the next ten years as we commemorate this important milestone.

Titles published so far are:

The Prepper Room by Karen Duve
Take Six: Six Portuguese Women Writers edited by Margaret Jull Costa
Take Six: Six Spanish Women Writers edited by Simon Deefholts & Kathryn Phillips-Miles
Slav Sisters: The Dedalus Book of Russian Women's Literature edited by Natasha Perova
Baltic Belles: The Dedalus Book of Estonian Women's Literature edited by Elle-Mari Talivee

The Madwoman of Serrano by Dina Salústio
Primordial Soup by Christine Leunens
Cleopatra Goes to Prison by Claudia Durastanti
The Girl from the Sea and other stories by Sophia de Mello Breyner Andresen
The Price of Dreams by Margherita Giacobino
The Medusa Child by Sylvie Germain
Days of Anger by Sylvie Germain
Venice Noir by Isabella Panfido
Chasing the Dream by Liane de Pougy
A Woman's Affair by Liane de Pougy
La Madre (The Woman and the Priest) by Grazia Deledda
Fair Trade Heroin by Rachael McGill
Co-wives, Co-widows byAdrienne Yabouza
Catalogue of a Private Life by Najwa Bin Shatwan
Baltic Belles: The Dedalus Book of Latvian Women's Literature edited by Eva Eglaja
This was the Man (Lui) by Louise Colet
This Woman, This Man (Elle et Lui) by George Sand
The Queen of Darkness (and other stories) by Grazia Deledda
The Christmas Present (and other stories) by Grazia Deledda
Cry Baby by Ros Franey
The Scaler of the Peaks by Karin Erlandsson
Take Six: Six Balkan Women Writers edited by Will Firth
My Father's House by Karmele Jaio

Forthcoming titles will include:

Take Six: Six Catalan Women Writers edited by Peter Bush
Take Six: Six Latvian Women Writers edited by Jayde Will

The Dedalus Book of Knitting: Blue Yarn by Karin Erlandsson
The Victor by Karin Erlandsson
Eddo's Souls by Stella Gaitano
Budapest Noir by Alison Langley
The Ridiculous Age by Margherita Giacobino

For more information contact Dedalus at
info@dedalusbooks.com

Take Six: Six Portuguese Women Writers edited by Margaret Jull Costa

'Few of Portugal's female novelists are to be found in English translation, which is as artistically regrettable as it is culturally telling. This collection of masterful short stories represents a notable and important stab at setting the record straight. Varied in style and subject, all the stories share a remarkable verve and freshness. Among the half-dozen writers selected is Agustina Bessa-Luís, who penned the 1954 classic A Sibila and whose death last year at the age of 96 provoked a day of official mourning in her adopted city of Porto. Aficionados of feminist literature should also check out New Portuguese Letters, whose erotic and irreverent subject matter saw it banned by the Salazar dictatorship. A worldwide cause celebre in its day, one of its three authors – Maria Velho da Costa – passed away late last month.'

Oliver Balch in *The Guardian*

£9.99   ISBN 978 1 910213 69 8   252p   B. Format

Take Six: Six Spanish Women Writers edited by Simon Deefholts & Kathryn Phillips-Miles

'Part of a wider collection bringing previously untranslated short stories to English-speaking audiences, *Take Six*'s opening author proves to be the ideal spokeswoman for its cause. Emilia Pardo Bazán's impassioned tone and uncompromising plots lay bare the very misogyny that has prevented her voice from being widely heard before now. And, like any girl group worth their salt, the authors that follow each add something fresh and distinctive to the mix.

Alongside Bazán's vehemence sit Carmen de Burgos' lyricism, Carmen Laforet's wistfulness, Cristina Fernández Cubas' surrealism, Soledad Puértolas' angst and Patricia Erlés' biting wit. Arranged chronologically according to the year of the authors' births, the volume doubles as an unexpectedly wonderful time machine, whisking the reader through over a century of changing styles, concerns and attitudes as it seeks to uncover a region of Spain's literary landscape where few British readers have ventured before.'

Rachel Rees in Buzz Magazine

£9.99   ISBN 978 1 912868 76 6   266p   B. Format

Portrait of a Family with a Fat Daughter by Margherita Giacobino

'This memoir of four generations of a family provides a vivid and eloquent picture of Italian life stretching from the late 19th century, when the peasant lifestyle had changed little from medieval times, up to the consumer culture of the 1950s. In writing about her female-dominated family, some of whom she is old enough to remember – most notably the matriarchal grandmother Ninin – Giacobino imbues her account with a real sense of intimacy. She has a powerful feel for traditional Italian culture, her early chapters conjuring up a time when the hierarchy of the family was the only true reality, fairness was unknown and "a moment's tenderness must last a week".'
Alastair Mabbutt in *The Herald*

'It's like a rural version of Elena Ferrante's Neapolitan saga. A powerful and atmospheric record of largely unexplored terrain.' Margaret Drabble in *The Times Literary Supplement*

'This sweeping narrative explores what it means to be Italian across oceans and historical epochs. Its vivid descriptions and deep cultural understanding leave a lasting mark.'
Italian Prose Award 2019 shortlist

£12.99   ISBN 978 1 910213 48 3   304p   B. Format

The Price of Dreams by Margherita Giacobino

Margherita Giacobino's book is a fictionalised biography/ autobiography of Patricia Highsmith, taking the form of diary entries supposedly written by her, interspersed with a third-person narrative. It focuses on her psychological and emotional life, with the emphasis on feelings, relationships and aspirations rather than facts, dates and events. A lesbian in an era when to be homosexual was to be reviled and discriminated against, and made to feel guilty and ashamed, Patricia Highsmith struggled with her sexual identity in this social context, and the book fruitfully explores how this might have contributed to her creative output.

The title is a reference to Patricia Highsmith's second novel *The Price of Salt*, a lesbian romance originally published under a pseudonym after it was rejected by the publisher of her first novel. It was not until 1990 that Patricia Highsmith agreed to its reissue under her own name, with the new title *Carol*.

'*The Price of Dreams* has captured something essential about Patricia Highsmith – a unique but altogether plausible version, whose voice so echoes the voices the woman created throughout her writing life. This is just an astonishing work – a revelation.'   Dorothy Allison

£12.99   ISBN 978 1 910213 95 7   336p   B. Format

Prague Noir (The Weeping Woman on the Streets of Prague) by Sylvie Germain

'An intricate, finely crafted and polished tale, *The Weeping Woman* brings magic-realism to the dimly lit streets of Prague. Through the squares and alleys a woman walks, the embodiment of human pity, sorrow, death. Everyone she passes is touched by her, and Germain skilfully creates an intense mood and feel in her attempt to produce a spiritual map of Prague.'   *The Observer*

'Firmly rooted in magic realism, Germain adds her own strain of dark romanticism and macabre imagination to create a tale poised between vision and elegy.'

Emily Dean in *The Sunday Times*

'Hallucinatory, lyrical in the extreme, it's a post-modernist playground for literary game-playing. It seems, at first, a radical departure for this gifted tale-teller but no, this is a teasing meditation on her familiar themes: history, place, creativity, death and desire.'   James Friel in *Time Out*

'The figure of this bereft woman develops into a memorable symbol: her sudden appearances – on a bridge, in a square, in a room – haunt the book like history, moved to tears.'

Robert Winder in *The Independent*

£8.99   ISBN 978 1 903517 73 4   112p   B. Format